THE

plague

THE
PLAGUE

by Joanne Dahme

RP|TEENS
PHILADELPHIA • LONDON

Printed in the United States

9   8   7   6   5   4   3   2   1
Digit on the right indicates the number of this printing

Library of Congress Control Number: 2008933264

ISBN 978-0-7624-3344-5

Photography by Steve Belkowitz
Cover and interior design by Frances J. Soo Ping Chow
Edited by Kelli Chipponeri
Typography: Bembo, Copperplate, and P22 Dearest

Running Press Teens is an imprint of
Running Press Book Publishers
2300 Chestnut Street
Philadelphia, PA 19103–4371

Visit us on the web!
www.runningpress.com

To my mother, who gave me her abundant enthusiasm
and to my father who shared his love of books.

—J.D.

prologue (1348 A.D.)

WHEN I WAS GEORGE'S AGE, I had an unsettling dream about Princess Joan, and this was at a time when the princess was a stranger to me, known only through a flashing glimpse from a faraway vantage point. As happens with so many dreams, I had lost most of the threads when I awoke. The dream returned to me as George and I lay amongst the king's soldiers in the woods of Bordeaux, a fractured reflection of our current predicament. I almost cried out against the injustice of the tardy omen.

In my dream, I was lost, separated from my mother as we visited the mobbed stalls of the marketplace. I was swept away by the crowd and somehow found myself deposited on the steps of a grand cathedral. The blast of a trumpet preceded the explosion of the cathedral's great wooden doors, which immediately expelled a procession of musicians, knights, and jesters, all colorfully costumed. I stood at the bottom of the steps, stunned by their beauty and grandeur, which was only eclipsed when the king and his family appeared. As I continued to stare senselessly, Princess Joan descended the few steps between us to stand in front of me.

"Are you alone, girl?" she asked. A gold crown studded with sparkling green stones lay upon her head. Her braided hair was draped over her left shoulder, like a sash upon her red velvet dress. She cocked her head at me and smiled. In my dream, I remember thinking it odd that the princess looked just like me.

"I am," I replied, blushing at my impudence of dreaming my own likeness on the princess's face.

The procession continued to move behind her but she took no notice.

"I would welcome your freedom," she said, clasping her hands as if to contain something that might fly away. "I am like a prisoner in my own castle, awaiting a marriage that will result in a new castle with the same constraints. Would you wear my crown for a day, so I may taste what you live daily?" she added hopefully.

I said nothing as she carefully lifted the crown from her head to place it on mine. Although she was gentle, I was shocked at the weight and discomfort of it and feared touching it, as it was not my own.

"I will meet you here on the morrow. For now, join the procession and carry yourself like a princess," she advised kindly. And then she scampered across the grass of the churchyard to join the mass of people that crowded the cobblestone street; her beautiful shimmering dress, for it sparkled a gleaming red in the sunlight, dissolved as she was swallowed by the throng within seconds.

I wanted to scream after her but I dared not. She was a princess and I was nothing but a beggar in comparison. I turned helplessly back toward the royal procession to observe the Black Prince withholding its progress with his gloved hand. "We must wait for the princess," he declared with a mocking smile, as the king and the prince's siblings paused at his bidding. He then extended his gloved hand to me. "Come along, sister. I would never abandon what is rightfully mine."

the pestilence

I STOOD ON THE DOCK, clutching a tied bundle of clothes beneath my arm. I closed my eyes, just for a minute, to see if I could still picture the four great ships, lined along the banks of the Thames like the powerful horses of the king's greatest knights. Their sails billowed at the hint of an August breeze. The king's red banner, with its three yellow lions frozen in mid-prowl, hung limply from the crow's nest of each. I opened my eyes. I was mesmerized by them, despite their familiarity, because for the first time in my life, my brother, George, and I would be leaving London to accompany Princess Joan to Bordeaux and I didn't know if we would ever return. The notion both frightened and thrilled me.

"George? Now where did he go?" I muttered to myself. I wasn't worried yet, as it looked to be at least another hour before sundown, when George and I were to board the princess's ship. George wanted to say good-bye to one of the shopkeepers whose stalls crowded the cobblestone plaza that spilled into the king's dock. Besides the princess, nine-year-old George was my entire family, as we had lost our parents to the pestilence a few years before, the last time it had invaded the city. My parents had told me that the fever invaded London like a fog and that the air we breathed allowed it to go from house to house, infecting almost everyone with the illness that bruised the body both inside and out until it burned the life from you.

George and I had somehow evaded the bad air, and thus, at fifteen, I was George's mother now, although he didn't quite see it that way. George was a strange boy, I thought, shaking my head. Sometimes I worried that what people said about him, that he was a bit daft, might be true.

I walked slowly to the riverbank, following the sound of the Thames as it slapped against the city's wooden bulkheads, as if affronted by the wall that separated it from the land. The air was damp and smelled heavily of fish and wet river grass, for the sun hadn't been visible for days. Barges filled with people and crates jammed the river, waiting for the tide to drop so they could pass easily under the bridge. Only one small boat seemed to make steady progress, its oarsman rhythmically pulling against the surface of the water. A man with his hands shackled sat in the bottom of the boat, his hooded head jerking with the movement of the oars. I felt a sudden chill. I had seen too many boats bearing prisoners make a trip to the Tower, the king's royal palace and fortress. It was said that those who went in by its river entrance, which led to the Tower's prison, were never seen again. I thought of George, who was always getting himself into some mischief. Perhaps it would be best if we never returned to London.

My father had said that the Thames offered many things, depending on your fortune in life. It fed our wells, provided fish and fowl for our tables, and floated the ships that carried silks, wines, spices, and other goods from distant lands. "What England cannot create, the Thames will provide passage for," he had told me, for he had unloaded many a ship when it reached the London port. But he had also heard that it was the foreign ships that had delivered the tainted airs of the pestilence.

I reminded myself that George and I had no cause for worry. The pestilence was gone, and although neither of us had ever sailed, Bordeaux was only a fortnight away. The princess told me that the king had promised it would be an easy trip across the channel to France. Three ships would be escorting the princess's vessel, each filled with the king's most powerful soldiers, "one hundred in all," she had added with a confident smile. The princess was to be married to Prince Pedro of the kingdom of Castile in Spain and she knew that her father wanted nothing to stand in the way of this wedding. The princess noted that the king was anxious to ensure that the Plantagenet line would rule in Spain as well as England and France.

"Nell, will you be boarding soon?" I heard a familiar voice call from behind. I turned and curtsied to Sir Robert Bourchier, the king's advisor who was also to join the princess on her journey. Sir Robert was a kind man who appeared to have a problem with his eyes whenever he encountered me. Often he would rub them, or squint, as if it were his eyes that placed the princess's likeness on my face. But despite these habits, which only I seemed to instigate, he was handsome and made royal by his choice of the rich blue tunics he wore that flashed purple against firelight.

"Yes, Sir Robert. I'm waiting for George. He should be here by sundown, when we were instructed to board the ship." I couldn't help but steal a glance past the quay. The pestilence had orphaned many children, and they were easy to spot in their tattered clothes as I watched them snaking among the adults' waists in the market, looking to steal a morsel. But I couldn't spy George.

Sir Robert looked at me quizzically. "You look worried, Nell. It is only when you furrow your brows do you temper your resemblance to the princess."

"I pray the princess never has a need for worry," I replied. "She should never be so burdened."

Sir Robert smiled, the creases around his eyes lending a kindness to his face. "Don't be too long, Nell, or the princess will be anxious for you."

I nodded. "Of course," I said politely as he turned on his heel toward the ship.

I looked back at the river and thought about the first time that I had been mistaken for the princess. It was probably both the best and worst day of our lives, a circumstance that cramped my stomach from this mixed dose of sorrow and salvation. In my mind, the day is as sharp as if it occurred yesterday, although it had happened almost two years before. George and I were standing outside our door, which had recently been marked with a large black cross. It had been raining, and a fine mist still wet the air. I remember looking down at our muddied feet as I heard the somber clang of the bell the gravediggers rang—a doomsday toll that had suffocated all other sounds for weeks—before they appeared with the cart. I grabbed George's hand as a big, dark man planted his fists on his hips and cursed at our slime-covered alley.

He stamped his foot before he pushed the boy toward our door. The boy slipped twice before reaching us. His clothes and face were streaked with dirt and his long brown hair pressed wet against his face and neck. He might have been a few years older than me, but he had the face of a cherub.

"Can you help me?" he asked, his voice trembling.

I said nothing and stared at the ground. I wanted no part of this. From the corner of my eye I saw two black rats leap from the pile of garbage that was growing beneath the window of a house a few doors away, as fresh contents were poured upon it daily.

The boy sighed before he pushed open our door. George tried to kick him but I yanked him against my stomach. By now, the man had managed to pull the cart to our door. He gave me a toothless smile.

"Sorry, girl. Is it your mother and your father, then?" he asked, cocking his head. George let out a tiny cry when he noticed the crumpled body already in the cart.

The man let go of the cart's handles and gently pushed George and I aside.

First they brought out Father, the boy carrying his legs and the man his arms. I didn't want to look at him. I wanted to remember Father as he had looked only weeks ago—brown and strong from his work under the sun on the banks of the Thames. Father was a fishmonger and had fed George and me a daily diet of his tales of the river life as well as the fish he caught. Now he was thin and the bones under his skin jutted out as if they were growing without the rest of his body. His clothes covered the sticky black sores that had grown under his arms.

Father had sworn that he had smelled the pestilence in the air as it rolled up the river during a particularly shrouded dawn, which had occurred only days before many of our neighbors began collapsing with the fever. Within a week, many had the painful black sores, which then caused nausea and the loss of one's bowels. Death was quick to follow and as difficult to evade as one's shadow. Father compared the pestilence with the plagues of Egypt that the monks talked about in the Bible. Horrible plagues of frogs, and locusts, and skin boils that God sent to earth to punish the Egyptians. Father said that the pestilence had invaded London before, but that this latest assault was particularly cruel and quick. Unlike the Egyptian plagues, God did not intervene to stop the pestilence.

"Don't look at him, George," I whispered as I covered George's eyes. They sort of swung Father's body into the cart. He settled awkwardly on the body beneath him.

Next they went in for Mother. I had meant to scream to George to close his eyes, to lock in the image of Mother as she was the last time we traveled to market. She had held our hands and pulled us beneath her apron as a team of ornery pigs scrambled through the narrow alleyway, pressing us against the peddlers' carts. Mother had laughed at our cries, her blue eyes mischievous yet her smile kind. I remember believing then that nothing could ever hurt us as long as we were encircled by Mother's loving arms.

What I did not want George to see was her once-beautiful face transformed into nothing but a skull with tangled blond hair, her gaze without interest or spark. I was ashamed that I had been afraid to close her eyes.

George and I followed the gravediggers to the road. I recalled feeling the coolness of the soft mud squishing through my toes. The old man and the boy were taking my parents to the church, to the pit that had been dug in the graveyard that would serve as the final resting place for hundreds. I thought George and I could stay with our parents there, unsure of where else to go.

The horses and soldiers approached as soon as the cart left our alley. The booming of the horses' hooves as they hit the cobblestone, solid with life and power, rekindled, for a moment, a hope that something could beat the pestilence. The soldier on the lead horse raised his arm to stop their progress, to allow the cart to pass. Even soldiers were afraid of such a death.

"Dear God," one of the men yelled. "It's the princess!"

I wondered if the man was crazed, although he appeared healthy enough and was richly dressed. A quick look around confirmed my suspicion that only the two gravediggers, and George and I, stood staring open-mouthed at the small army in front of us.

I peered at the man who dared to cry out as if the cart were invisible, surprised by his outburst, as nobody paid any attention to anything here but the death. He was astride a huge white horse, from which he leaned forward to look intently at me. His face was covered by a thick red beard flecked with white, as was his hair, which fell in tangles around his shoulders. The skin of his face was pocked yet his eyes shone with a brazen vigor. Both the man and the horse were covered with a mantle of red decorated with yellow lions. The man wore a golden crown.

"You look exactly like my daughter, even if it is my daughter in one of my worst nightmares. Are your parents dead?" he asked.

Still I could only stare until George nudged me in my ribs with his bony elbow. "He's talking to you," he whispered.

I took a deep breath. "I'm sorry for my rudeness, sir," I replied, wondering if I should curtsy. "Only the death carts travel these alleys." I was taken aback by his appearance here and I struggled to speak respectfully. Yet my voice rang meek in my ears. This man was wearing a crown. But why would someone from the royal family pass by our pestilence-filled alley? "Indeed, it has come for my parents," I finally acknowledged.

"I am sorry, child. I'm afraid that not even your king can conquer the pestilence," he said, "although I have vowed to do my best. This plague, if sent by God, does not bear a clear message as to my kingdom's transgressions. I know not what to right." He smiled bitterly as he turned to look at his soldiers, as if acknowledging their swords were but feathers against the air.

George grabbed my hand and I gasped involuntarily. Could this man be our king?

The gravediggers flinched at the pronouncement. They must have come to the same astonishing conclusion as George and me. We all plunged into a fearful silence. The only sound heard was the soft scraping of the window shutters in the houses surrounding us, squeaking in protest like house rats against their timid movements. Our neighbors—the ones that still survived—feared the death cart. But having a chance to gaze furtively upon a bearded king was a different matter.

"Are you the king?" George asked breathlessly.

I sucked in the tainted air.

"Indeed I am," the king replied, a touch of melancholy in his tone. "Are you her brother?" The king raised his chin in my direction, and for a brief moment, his face softened.

"He is, sir," I replied, shamed at the thought of allowing George to carry this burden of speaking to our king. "Although I think I am his mother now," I added softly.

This brought an amused smile to the king's face.

"I offer a promise to you, child, if you are willing to

make a vow to me in return," he stated, reaching to pat his horse's thick neck as the creature began to nervously stamp its feet.

The gravedigger boy turned to look at me, his eyes wide in his dirt-streaked face. He then mouthed, "Say something."

"A-anything, my lord," I stammered.

He nodded, satisfied. The three soldiers flanking him glanced at one another as if unsure of the king's intent.

He turned to appraise them, causing all three to stiffen in their saddles. "These men," he said, waving his hand in their direction, "are a part of the royal guard and can protect my children with their weapons and skills. What they cannot provide is a natural cunning," he said, shaking his head as if his soldiers were remiss. Two of them looked stricken. One placed his hand on the hilt of his sword.

"But you, my dear, bear the face of my daughter, Princess Joan. Through your own countenance, and your willingness to serve as her best protection, you can keep her from harm better than any weapon in my kingdom. If you pledge to do this, I will have you and your brother escorted to my castle in Windsor, to live with us as my daughter's servants." He cocked his head, waiting for my reply.

George squeezed my hand again, hard enough now to crush its bones. The gravedigger boy turned to look at me once more. Before he could prod me, for I didn't need his prodding, I replied. "Of course, my lord. It will be an honor."

"Very good," he said with gusto. Turning to the soldier on his right, he commanded, "Take this girl and her brother to the pest house."

The soldier wrinkled his nose and sneered at us in disgust.

"If they are still alive in a fortnight, I expect you to deliver them to me, clean and unmolested," he added ominously.

It was then that I remembered my parents in the death cart and my stomach soured with shame at my speedy abandonment of them.

Since that fateful day, from which two years have passed, I have been told how much the princess and I resemble each other. Despite her royal birth and my poor one, we could easily pass as sisters, if not twins. When I stared into the princess's clear green eyes, her beauty often startled me. How could I possibly be compared to the princess? I felt my cheekbones as I allowed my mouth to mirror the princess's generous smile.

Her lips were full and colored cherry with ochre. Her

nose was thin and sculpted flawlessly between high cheekbones. Her eyes were luminous and heavily lashed. And she wore her long, thick, light brown hair woven in braids that she bore like a crown. She was tiny of waist and ankle and carried herself with the grace of a swan. To gaze upon the princess was at risk of losing one's breath. And yet her heart was generous and did not overly acknowledge the beauty that housed it.

The king had lingered in front of the death cart, as he had seen a reflection of his daughter in me. And yet when I traced my own face and body, I remembered the sun marks that lightly sprinkled my own cheeks and the nose that still bore a perceptible jag from a break. My own body was lithe and strong but was denied a natural grace. I could throw an apple one hundred yards, but I could not balance it on my head.

The last time I had dismissed the idea of our similarities, the princess had picked up a looking glass, held it under her chin, and pointed it at me. I blinked back at the young woman with the brown hair falling across her shoulders, her cheeks burnished by sun or embarrassment. I gazed again at the princess and returned her satisfied smile. Perhaps we were twinned, and the differences only apparent to my own critical eyes.

"Nell!"

I swung around to watch George push his way through the crowd, using his shoulders or arms to nudge wider hips and waists aside. His black tunic made his bare arms look white and thin, almost skeletal, I thought with a pang, and the boots he wore were oversized and ill fitting. He clomped against the cobblestones, constantly changing course, as an old woman at one of the stalls lurched across her table to catch a jostled apple and a man carrying a heavy bag of his wares turned a full circle to avoid knocking George on his head.

"George, what is that in your hand?" I asked suspiciously as he collided into my leg, giving it a hug. I tugged on a handful of sweaty blond hair. Someone had given him a ragged trim around the ears. "What have you been doing?" I asked more sternly.

George raised his face to mine, gave me a big smile, and exposed his two missing teeth. The light in his blue eyes was doing a jig.

"Well," he started. "I had my hair cut for our journey and said good-bye to John Moore. I want to look presentable for the princess's wedding." He nodded, proud of his words. He knew I couldn't disagree on that point.

"John Moore?" I pressed. He was a blacksmith who

befriended George after we moved to live with the princess. John was burly and gruff in manner but, lacking his own son, had found a soft spot for George, always giving him his cast-off pieces. As a result, George swore he was going to apprentice with the blacksmith someday. "What did he give you?"

George opened his hand slowly as if releasing a firefly. "He gave us an amulet," he whispered proudly. "To protect us from the pestilence. John had it blessed by the parish priest."

I peered more closely at the round metal piece in George's hand. The outline of some sort of animal had been scratched into its surface. I felt a chill.

"What is that, George?" I shifted my bundle of clothes and ran my fingertip across it.

"Why, it's a rat, of course. A black rat!" he added. "John says that if I wear this around my neck, it will protect me and those I love. I love you, Nell."

"Hmmm," was my only reply. What could a blacksmith know about charms, even if they were blessed? I doubted he would still be a blacksmith if he had such knowledge. But George cared for him. I resisted the impulse to take the thing away from him.

"Nell! George! You had better come aboard!" I turned

toward the river. Sir Robert was waving us toward the ship. He had escorted the princess aboard, and they were now standing on the deck, surrounded by a knot of soldiers in leather and armor plates, longbows in their hands. One of the soldiers was aiming an arrow at the sky, as if he might shoot for the missing sun. When he released it, it soared toward the heavens, then paused, as if surprised by the loss of its power. It fell into the river like an injured bird.

I grabbed George's sweaty hand as I kept my eye on the princess. I had made it a habit to study her every detail, as I took the king's charge seriously. The princess was wearing her dark purple silk gown, covered with little golden stars. It was like gazing at the midnight sky. Her hair was braided and wrapped around her head like a crown.

George and I headed for the gangplank. "Slip that amulet around your neck and under your tunic," I mumbled to him. I didn't think the princess would be pleased with the blacksmith's efforts.

George and I shared a straw mattress in a corner of the princess's bedroom. The princess had seen to it that the mattress was covered with a rainbow of richly colored quilts, some of them gifts from royal families across the channel, saving us from an itchy night's sleep. I could hear the princess breathing softly. She had been nervous and excited as we left the dock. I was glad now that she could sleep.

The air smelled like fresh-cut hay and I listened lazily to the wooden ship creak like an old man's rocking chair as it headed first to Portsmouth and then on to Bordeaux. As I lay in the dark, allowing my body to feel each rise and fall of the ship, I wondered where our journey would lead us. The king's ships were bound to eventually return home filled with bolts of silken cloth and caskets of red wine. George and I would stay with the princess once she married Prince Pedro, and the three of us would become members of a very different kingdom.

Suddenly I felt George's fingernails digging into my forearm.

"George!" I hissed quietly, not wanting to wake up the princess. "Stop it! That hurts."

"Listen, Nell," he begged, his voice tinged more with curiosity than fear. "Do you hear the scratching?"

I sat up and tried to look around the room, but I couldn't see anything in the blackness, not even George's face. I tilted my head, straining to listen. "Stop breathing," I whispered to him. I heard George take a gulp of air and then nothing.

I did hear it. The sound of something hard scraping against the wooden floor. It wasn't a big noise, so I figured whatever was making the noise wasn't very big. The sound was coming from outside our door.

"Nell, I think it's a rat," George said, running out of breath. He practically spit out the last word.

"A rat!" Now it was my turn to dig my nails into George. I hated rats—the way they scurried into dark corners like evil spirits. Rats had been everywhere when my parents died—in our house, our alley. They hadn't feared the death.

Suddenly George was leaning over me, grinding his elbow into my thigh.

"What are you doing?" I asked nervously. I didn't want George bounding up to catch the creature.

"I'm pointing my amulet at the rat," he answered, as if that was the most practical thing to do. "This will keep it away from us."

The scratching did stop, and we both held our breath as we waited to see if it would start again.

A glow of light appeared in the hallway, slipping into our room through the small space beneath the door. The light seemed to jiggle as if someone was swinging a lantern.

George and I pulled back against the sound of approaching footsteps. I clasped my hand over his mouth as we both cringed when we heard the creature squeal and then fall silent.

amulet

WE ARRIVED IN PORTSMOUTH on Thursday, sailing into its harbor, which was alive with light. Brigades of the king's best soldiers were there, having recently scoured this section of England, upon the king's orders, to assess the wrath of his kingdom's plague. It was around noontime, for I could feel the heat of the sun resting on my head like my father's hand. The surface of the water glittered as it was dappled with sunbeams, and the gulls that had been following our small fleet were swooping hungrily at the small fish dancing in our wake. The docks were crowded with other great ships, and well-muscled men wrestled with crates of wine, or cloth, or other treasures from faraway places. Women and children lined the docks in welcome, waving to the men, perhaps anxious for the return of a loved one or the chance to scavenge spilled contents. Their whoops and cries mingled with those of the gulls. The scene made George smile, and I knew he must have been feeling as merry as I.

As we approached the seawall, a cluster of soldiers stood on the dock, surrounding the king's ambassador, Sir Andrew Ullford, who had spent the last month in Portsmouth, preparing for the journey. He looked tiny, like a newly apprenticed page, nestled among the long swords and pieces of armor that the soldiers carried. Sir Andrew, white-haired and red-nosed, was clothed in an unassuming brown tunic and stockings and appeared oblivious to the jostling of the soldiers around him. He wore a serious expression on his face, and I knew him well enough to assume that he was mentally reviewing his list of duties. Sir Andrew was extremely forgetful, but was trusted by the king. George was fascinated by Sir Andrew and liked to watch him walk in his "memory circles," as Sir Andrew called the pacing he did when he struggled to remember a forgotten task.

Our ship bumped against the pilings as the aroma of roasting pig engulfed us.

"Yum," George said, grabbing my hand. "Should we

follow the scent and get us some food?"

I could see the gray smoke rising from one of the stalls in the port's market, and a woman with an apron tied around her waist shooing some children away. "It looks as if Portsmouth beat us to it." I laughed.

As soon as we dropped anchor, the deck was swarming with soldiers greeting their fellow knights. Their eyes looked alive with the thoughts of foreign battle, and they slapped one another on the back or shoulder as if their affection could only be shared in a hearty touch. George was staring at them adoringly.

"Princess?" Sir Andrew hesitated in front of me and began to do a slow bow until I shook my head.

"No, Sir Andrew. It is I, Nell. The princess is with the tailor, trying on her wedding dress one more time." I curtsied at him. I was only doing my duty but I often felt duplicitous wearing one of the princess's old dresses. This one was a beautiful green silk with gold and red roses embroidered on the sleeves and around the neckline.

"So it is." Sir Andrew smiled, his watery blue eyes looking soft against his weathered face. "I should have known, of course, with the little one bobbing like a goose around you."

I tried to suppress my own smile as I instinctively

reached for George. He didn't like to be teased and there was no telling how he would react. His latest trick had been the placement of a live toad in a pot of the castle's cook, who had a habit of calling him "Little Galahad" because of George's obsession with magical amulets, ancient relics, and religious artifacts. George didn't hear Sir Andrew's comment, as he was still staring at the soldiers. I turned when I heard one of them address Sir Andrew.

"Sir Robert wished me to ask if you have heard any rumors about the pestilence."

Sir Andrew's red face suddenly drained of its color. I felt my own stomach tighten.

"The pestilence?" he croaked. "In France?"

The soldier impatiently brushed his long black hair over his shoulder. "Yes. Sir Robert heard of burnings in some of the smaller ports from a group of wine merchants making their way to London. Nothing they had seen with their own eyes, though."

Sir Andrew shook his head slowly. "We received no news in Windsor of such a plague in France. It can't be true," he insisted in disbelief. "Nonetheless, when we reach Bordeaux, I wish to send out a party before we anchor." He then blessed himself.

The soldier nodded and led Sir Andrew to the cabins below. I jumped when George tugged on my sleeve.

"Nell, my amulet is strong enough to protect you, me, and the princess. But what about the others? What about the soldiers? I don't think it is powerful enough for us all."

I touched him lightly on the chin to make him look at me. He found it easier to tell me stories when he didn't have to look into my eyes. "That's not our worry, George. We must leave that up to God and the king. Besides"—I smiled, despite my own gnawing little doubt—"the soldier was only sharing a rumor."

"Maybe," George replied, his mouth pursed, unconvinced. "But I think I will ask Father Paul. Maybe he can do a special blessing."

"Really?" I tried not to sound too surprised. George didn't like Father Paul, who was traveling with us so that the princess could still receive her sacraments. Father Paul was always telling George what a sinful little boy he was. I didn't like Father Paul either. He never appeared happy.

"Fine, George. You go see Father Paul, while I check on the princess. I won't be long," I promised.

I should have suspected something in that gap-toothed smile, for when I returned to the deck, one of the soldiers, a young one who reminded me of the gravedigging boy who came for my parents, stepped in front of me. This boy really a young man with a child's mischievous gleam in his eyes smiled in amusement, though.

"Your brother has left the ship, little princess," he said with mock respect. The soldiers called me many variations of "princess." They thought my job was a poor one, but I didn't have time to challenge this particular soldier now.

"Did you see where he went?" I asked. "I was told we will leave port by morning." I hated that my voice quivered, but George could disappear for hours. What if he got lost?

His own voice softened as he pointed in the direction of a church spire that rose above the roofs of the town. Its bell began to toll as we spoke. "He ran down that road, bumping into people for as far as I could follow him with my eyes. He's an unsteady one."

"Thank you," I said, heading toward the gangway. I knew I shouldn't leave the ship dressed as the princess, but I was not about to leave George behind.

"Wait!" the soldier called from behind. "You can't go into town alone. Not like that," he added.

"Then come with me," I called. "I must go after George."

I followed the church spire like a beacon in the darkness, as I feared losing my way, the paths and houses and shops leaning in toward me foreign and nothing but obstacles in my quest to find George. I avoided the stares of the people who parted to provide me with passage as I tripped over cobblestones and gutters. Their alarmed curt-sies or awkward bows only impeded my progress.

"Make way for the princess," a voice bellowed behind me. I turned to see the young soldier by my side, his sword drawn to encourage the people to give us space. He winked at me.

"You wouldn't dare do that to the princess," I said, trying to sound nettled.

"Make way, make way," he continued, undeterred. I stole a glimpse of his face, and indeed it had the rounded cheeks and chin of that sorry boy, the boy who had reminded me of a cast-out angel, but this soldier was cocky and handsome in a rough way. For a moment, I wished that he had tied his long brown hair at the nape of his neck so that I could better inspect his face.

We stopped when we reached a stone wall. The cobblestone alley spilled west into the small courtyard of the church. There I spied George, gazing, trembling, as his fingers clutched the black iron bars of the church's graveyard. Other men and women had their faces pressed up against the gate, which kept them out of the grassy area reserved for the dead. They were yelling at the priest and his assistants, who toiled on the cemetery side of the gate. The iron bars were no defense against the harsh taunts and desperate pleas. Caged hens at the peddlers' stalls were the object of more reverence.

"Fool!" a man in a dirty tunic and rent stockings screamed from the courtyard. His hair was knotted and his bearded face was red from the sun. "You will curse us all."

A woman with two young children clutching her skirts pleaded, "Please, Father, you will scare us all to death."

I slipped behind George. The priest and his men had shovels in their hands. A number of pits had been dug where there was room between the tombstones. The pit nearest the priest was dark, as the soil beneath the grass was still moist. A few of the other pits that pockmarked the ground were deep, as I could not see the bottom from where we stood. Their dirt walls were dusty, already bleached by the sun.

"George," I whispered, shaking him by the shoulder and not wanting to startle him. "What are you doing here?"

He turned to look into my face. His blue eyes were wide with fear. "I wanted the priest to bless the amulet, to make it stronger."

"Little princess, we should go back to the ship," the young soldier interrupted. He was standing behind us, his sword still drawn. His voice sounded suddenly urgent. The scene before us had caused me to forget him.

I nodded and tugged at George to make him move. "George, let go of the bars," I ordered, but it was too late. The priest had spied us.

"Wait!" he called as he walked, dragging his shovel in his wake. His assistants stood by their pit, leaning on theirs, as if these breaks occurred all the time. His gait was odd, probably due to the slight hump on his back. He was bald with a fuzz of hair around both ears. His robe was covered in dust.

"He walks like a crab," George cried, a bit too loudly. The people who stood on the outskirts of the graveyard suddenly crowded around us, curious as to what the priest would say. Our soldier motioned them away with his sword.

The priest stood directly across from us now, on the other side of the bars, and wiped the sweat from his brow with his sleeve. He narrowed his bloodshot eyes.

"Why are you digging these pits?" I asked. My heart was trembling. No one else said a word. The priest stared at us and then spat before answering.

"I've heard from my friends that the pestilence is in France. It's just a matter of time before it reaches England." He was shouting so all could hear him. "We weren't prepared last time. The dead outnumbered us."

"What friends?" George asked, truly interested. "Do you mean the angels?"

"George!" I said under my breath, for I was sure the priest would take his question as jest.

The priest stumbled a last step and, grabbing a bar, slid down so that his face was peering straight into George's.

"You could say that, my boy," he wheezed, as if out of breath from the effort. He smelled of earth and sweat. "The angels come to me in dreams. I saw the fires in France. They are everywhere."

"He's a heretic!" someone yelled. "Or he's playing with the devil," another voice replied. The hecklers were all dressed shabbily. The people standing near them backed away. They seemed more hesitant to attack a priest, even if the weapons were mere words.

But the priest dismissed them with a wave of his hand. I yanked at George again as he struggled to pull his amulet from his tunic.

The crowd started to press close again, curious to see what George was doing.

Our soldier grabbed my arm and practically lifted me off the ground. "We are going," he commanded. "Grab the brat or leave him."

I clutched George by the arm just as roughly as the soldier was holding me.

"Wait!" he pleaded as he held the amulet in his hand. He pointed it at the priest. "I want you to bless this, so it will protect the king's soldiers from the pestilence. All except that one," he added, scowling at our soldier.

"Are you daft, boy?" our soldier accused. "This priest is cursed with visions. Leave him!"

I saw the priest's eyes widen as he scanned the amulet and mouthed the word "rat." He ignored the soldier as he thrust his bony hand out as if to grab it. As I watched in horrified fascination, two black rats scampered suddenly across the graveyard and leaped onto a gravestone, just yards behind the priest. They paused, balancing themselves, their noses and whiskers twitching, as if to see what the priest would do.

I grabbed George by the hand and yelled, "Go!" to the soldier, who turned to clear our escape path. He held me by the arm as we ran, George begging us to go back for the blessing.

The priest's voice boomed at our backs. "Lord have

mercy on us. For we are sinners and have earned the wrath of heaven!"

I took one glance back to see the crowd dispersing. Some shook their heads, some covered their ears or mouth. Others nervously blessed themselves, just as Sir Andrew had earlier that morning.

The princess had given us a good scolding when we returned to the ship. She had been waiting on the deck, with the short, round Father Paul beside her. I observed the soldiers' amused looks as they leaned against the deck rails, enjoying the entertainment. George actually gave them a shy little wave, so pleased he was that they even noticed him.

I felt ashamed as the princess gently reminded me of my rank and duty. I squeezed George's bony hand— squeezed it hard—to share my discomfort. Despite George's whimper and Father Paul's indignant frown, the princess remained serene. Her green eyes showed kindness and her face remained soft, absent of the hard lines of anger.

"You are like a sister to me, Nell. You sacrificed your freedom to do as you please when you swore your allegiance to me." She said this a bit wistfully, as if sensitive to this price. "It is nearly dark and you must stay safe," she said, causing Father Paul to pull on his brown robe distractedly. The princess turned to George. "And you, young one. It is your task to protect your sister, so that she can better protect us all."

"But that was exactly what I was trying to do!" George burst out. "I wanted the parish priest to bless my amulet." He held it up. The amulet dangled from its crude iron chain for all to see. The princess barely looked at it as she addressed Father Paul.

"You can bless it, I'm sure, Father. Why don't we plan the blessing after morning services," she instructed rather than asked.

Father Paul sputtered as he examined the amulet still swaying in front of George's face. He frowned in disdain. "If that is your wish, princess."

Before she returned to her quarters, she commended our "gallant" soldier, Henry, who proclaimed his name as he basked in the glow of her appreciation. How smart it was for him to follow us, she praised. When she nodded to Father Paul that she was ready to descend to her quarters, Henry gave me another quick wink. The impudence.

The remainder of our two-week journey was uneventful, except for one of the last evenings on ship. I couldn't sleep and I felt I was suddenly suffocating, my heart chasing the thoughts running through my head. I had crept from my bed to get some air on deck, careful not to wake the princess or George. I grabbed my cloak as I knew the nighttime sea air was cool.

Suddenly I missed England and the Castle in Windsor. While lying in my bed, I began to worry that my memories of my mother and father would be left behind, buried with them in the graveyard with nothing to mark their existence but a stark wooden cross shared by hundreds.

We were going to Bordeaux, and then on to Castile to live. I knew nothing of these lands or the ways of their people. How would I protect George and the princess when I didn't know what to protect them from? It was then that I felt the ghostly hands that always seemed to press against my chest when I had such thoughts.

The deck was deserted, with the exception of a few soldiers on watch. They leaned against the rails or masts and struggled to fight off the urge to doze as tempted by the gentle swaying of the ship.

I pulled my cloak around me and walked barefoot to the rear deck. We had lost sight of Portsmouth after only a few hours of journey. Now all I could see was the ocean as dark as a raven's wing sliced white by our ship. The moon, almost full, illuminated the ocean's surface, proving how lonely it was out here. The boundless ocean made me want to cry, for I suddenly felt small and weak. Must not everyone feel this when they are on the sea? Only the king's three other ships, one on each side of us, a bit more than a stone's throw away, and the last, trailing in our wake, attested that we were not completely abandoned.

It was then that I heard a high-pitched tinkling, a sound that reminded me of the bells of jesters, frenzied and staccato as they danced with abandon in the royal processions. I glanced at the stairs that led belowdecks. The sound was not coming from there. I cocked my head and realized it was coming from the sea. I held my breath. I had heard the tales the soldiers told about the ships lost to their waters, their crews crushed beneath the drowning weight of the waves to spend eternity haunting the living who dared to sail. They had whispered about the sharp, strangled cries, the tragic last gasps of those dragged to the sea bottom by the bulk of their armor. Or by the grasp of some unseen creature, they added when they knew George or I was listening. They had never mentioned bells.

It rang again and someone called, the angry words lost to the salty air. Suddenly, the soldiers on watch jumped to their feet and swore as they clambered to the portside and drew their swords, still a little clumsy from sleep. I watched as they peered over the side, my heart thumping at the unknown terror that called to them. And then I heard the angry cuss and the soldiers sheathed their swords at their sides again. "My lord," they mumbled as they bowed their heads.

My lord? The idea was incredulous. It couldn't be the king. I crept back and hid behind the mast as the soldiers heaved a dark figure onto the deck. He was taller and thinner in figure than the soldiers and wore a hood on his tunic that hid his face. It was only when he turned toward the moon that I caught a glimpse of his profile—the sharp nose, the recessed eyes, and the ebony beard that he wore to a point like his shoes. It was the Black Prince.

"Princess!" he called. He was known for his hawklike vision. My heart exploded as I stepped from my sorry hiding place and curtsied.

"It is Nell, my prince," I whispered. "I could not sleep."

He pulled off his hood as he walked over to me, a bit unsteady on his feet still. The soldiers stood along the rail, not knowing what to do next.

He lifted my chin, his fingernails grazing my cheek. I made myself look into his dark eyes, hooded even more in the shadows of the silver light.

"My, you could pass for my sister so readily." The ice in his voice made me shiver.

"I do not have her wisdom or beauty, my lord," I insisted.

"And so loyal." He smiled, his chin growing longer with the act. "I will expect the same allegiance for the princess's brother.

"Of course, my lord." My face was burning. I feared the prince, as many did. The tales of his cruelty in battle were shared heartily by the soldiers. I was glad it was dark.

And then, just as quickly, he dismissed me, turning his back and calling to the soldiers to collect his things and bring them to his quarters.

I watched them descend, the prince in the middle of his single line of knights, the last one throwing a sack over his shoulder as he stood in queue. I wondered why the prince had appeared in the middle of the night and from seemingly nowhere. I blinked in the moonlight, for a moment swearing that I could see the sack ripple with movement.

bordeaux

THE BLACK PRINCE barely acknowledged me during the remaining days of our journey. He kept close to his quarters. Only his bell, which would clatter off-key, as if it were cracked, served as a reminder that the prince was with us. He would ring it many times a day, whenever he felt the least discomfort from a hungry stomach or the threat of boredom. One morning I discovered George with his ear to the prince's door, and my heart took a leap. The prince would have thrown him overboard if he caught my brother spying, of this I was sure. George protested that he wasn't trying to be sneaky, he was trying to figure out what was making the nervous squeaking sound. "I never heard the prince make that sort of noise," he said.

The princess was delighted that her oldest brother had joined her on her bridal journey. Since the king had announced the princess's impending marriage to the prince of Castile, the prince had fawned on her, lavishing her with praise and advice on her future role as queen. Before her betrothal, I had never witnessed the prince take much notice of his sister, so I could not help but to wonder about this sudden interest. The princess, however, welcomed this new affection. There was a marked change in behavior among the soldiers and the ship's crew. Their earlier, lighthearted demeanor was gone. Even the rascal Henry dared not divert his attention to making sport.

But the prince could be charming. I watched as he shared a meal in our quarters with the princess, while Sir Robert and Sir Andrew reviewed the princess's itinerary once we arrived in Bordeaux. The prince raved anew about his sister's beauty and her triumphant betrothal to Prince Pedro, telling her that together they would ensure the rule of the Plantagenet dynasty in Europe. Then, after she clapped her hands in delight over his attention, he would turn to the senior diplomats and tease them, imitating their mannerisms unmercifully. Sir Andrew would smile indulgently, but Sir Robert seemed to smolder beneath his restrained manner.

I forgot my misgivings about the prince as we drew closer to Bordeaux. This was the king's land in the French territory of Gascony. I had heard the princess tell stories of her brother's bravery in battles at Crecy and Calais. England may have a smaller population than France, but it has more money and is expert in the arts of battle, she shared proudly. The king handsomely paid peasants and soldiers from many countries to wage his battles in France. These soldiers of the king wielded new weapons called longbows, which terrorized the horses, if not the men of the French infantry. I myself had seen our soldiers practice with these weapons. Their metal-tipped arrows could be released in rapid succession, like waves lapping against the bulkheads of the Thames in the wake of a ship. Their deadly arc propelled them hundreds of yards farther than the arrows of the crossbow. As a result of these battles and the soldiers who continued to fight them on behalf of the king, the king already owned parts of France, and his daughter, soon to be married to the prince of Castile, would allow the king to claim as his own the land of the Iberian Peninsula, too. It was said that the prince rejoiced in the terror wrought upon France and was as impatient as his father to expand the realm of the Plantagenet kingdom. Although I was uncomfortable with wars, particularly when I thought about the death they wrought, it made me feel safe that the princess and George and I were protected by the most powerful army in the world.

The soldiers on our ship had shared some of their own battle tales and spoke reverently of the Black Prince's dark armor and black heart. In battle, they would say, the king and his sons were expected to lead their army to victory without the weakness of mercy. I thought about George and knew that I would want the prince to do whatever was necessary to keep him safe.

I found my heart hammering as we approached the fog-shrouded port of Bordeaux. George had been standing beside me on deck as we entered its misty waters. I heard him draw in his breath.

"It looks full of spirits," he exclaimed. Indeed it did.

"All castles have that heavenly appearance at dawn," I asserted, although our castles at home didn't seem to rise from the waters.

The sailors whistled to alert one another that we were drawing close. The soldiers on watch joined us on the bow. No one spoke.

The white stones of the king's castle—le Chateau de l'Ombriere—seemed to glow against the dark cliffs overshadowing the port. It could serve as a beacon to our ship, except the castle appeared besieged and deserted. The air tasted like vinegar.

I could sense an odd foreboding settling on us, as if the fog were dampening our spirits. We all squinted into the gloom, as if trying to make out whatever was tainting our excitement.

I could see the crenellated walls of the castle that zigzagged across the treacherous cliff. The castle's watch-towers seemed to float above them, separated from their walls by wisps of clouds. Surely there were soldiers pacing the wall walks, with bows in hand. We were just too far away to see them.

"Its drawbridge is up," George said, breaking the silence. "That isn't a very welcoming sign." His voice was thin with worry.

"And there are no other ships in the harbor besides our own," I added distractedly, not meaning to say my thoughts aloud.

"Nonsense!" a voice chided from behind.

I turned to see the Black Prince joining our little band as he impatiently waved a hand at us. He was wearing a black tunic and stockings. Unlike his peers and diplomats who preferred multicolored garments, the prince always wore black. Only the gold-threaded belt slung about his waist provided some relief to his somber appearance. Although his eyes were bloodshot, his movements and voice sounded fresh.

"Are you trying to scare my soldiers, Nell?" He was standing beside me now, speaking right into my ear.

"No, sir." I curtsied. "I was just surprised by the emptiness of the port. Perhaps it is still early," I noted, feeling the stares of the soldiers, who seemed rooted to their places.

Suddenly I felt George squirming between us.

"Shouldn't the ships be anchored, though? There are always ships anchored at ports," he reasoned.

The Black Prince glowered at George for a moment and then abruptly laughed. "You remind me of a bothersome rat, boy, always able to squeeze into the tiniest crevice. Tell me why you are on this journey," he instructed while plucking at his beard.

"I am with Nell," he protested, glancing at the soldiers, as if they would intervene.

"As you know, he is my brother, my liege. I am responsible for him until he is of age," I said. I was trembling, but I didn't know if it was from fear or anger or perhaps a mixture of both. How I abhorred this prince, even though I knew that I shouldn't. He was my king's heir, appointed by God. He was also our protector.

"I see," he replied gravely. "Are you superstitious, Nell?" he asked. His hand was resting on George's tousled hair. Its veins welled up as he flexed his fingers. I sensed that he was feeling just how easy it would be to crush George's skull.

"No I am not, my lord," I replied with too much emotion. I needed to get George away from him.

"My lord, look! The drawbridge is coming down." We all turned to see Henry, who had at some point joined our party. He was pointing to the castle, looking eager to please his prince. He was not in his armor yet. In his dusty tunic and loose stockings he looked more like a boy.

The Black Prince scowled. "So they have. Of course they have. They must see our banners!" And then he turned on his heel to return to his quarters. He stopped for a moment to shout one last order. "Make sure the princess is ready, Nell. She needs to look glorious this morning."

"I will," I whispered, for he was already descending the stairs.

I knew something was terribly wrong as we stood on the lowered drawbridge, waiting for the castle's gate-keepers. As the spiked iron portcullis was slowly raised, a small terror gnawed at my guts. The Black Prince had instructed Sir Andrew to accompany our party to determine if the castle was fit for its royalty. Fifteen soldiers, including Henry, now dressed in his ill-fitting armor, surrounded Sir Andrew, George, and me. I was wearing the princess's green silk dress again and couldn't help worrying as George kept stepping on its hem. I was loath to say anything to him, as he had been making nervous sounds ever since we left the ship.

The portcullis screamed against the effort to raise it, as if denying our right of entry. *Surely the castle could not know that I am a fake.* I could barely make out the figure of the armored gatekeeper on the other side of the tower's arch. He waved us through and, in the mist, looked like one of the lost spirits I imagined at sea.

Sir Andrew cleared his throat and took me by the arm. "Let us go through, Nell, though I dislike the quiet on the other side of this tower."

I bit my lip and nodded as I pulled at my skirt. George was walking beside me now, staring up at the ceiling.

"Just looking at the murder holes. I don't want some ill-tempered soldiers thinking they can just drop rocks or boiling liquids on our heads," he explained. His remark caused our soldiers to raise their own sights.

Sir Andrew laughed nervously. "This is the king's castle, boy. These soldiers are *our* soldiers," he said kindly, almost as if he were reminding himself of his whereabouts.

"Sir Andrew," I asked quietly, "Why does the castle appear so empty? There is no one in the courtyard save the gatekeeper." I was glad that the princess was still on board our ship. We crossed the second drawbridge and I caught the scent of the moat. It smelled like sickness to me. Sir Andrew held his purse to his nose.

"I don't know, Nell. I don't like this stillness either," he replied, squinting suspiciously around the courtyard. "The mayor of Bordeaux should be here to receive us, as he oversees the castle on the king's behalf." Sir Andrew patted my arm and continued. "Don't you worry about anything but playing the princess."

I nodded as the toothless gatekeeper approached us. He was dragging his right leg as if it were a body. I flinched when I noticed that a portion of his skull was flattened.

"Quite a daunting greeting," Sir Andrew sniffed as the gatekeeper bowed. "Where is the remainder of your defense?"

The gatekeeper stole a look at George and at the young soldiers surrounding us. Our soldiers scowled fiercely as their hands gripped their sword hilts.

"A nervous lot, aren't you? Not a comforting entourage for the princess," the old man scolded. "We are not under siege. Our soldiers are walking the battlements." He pointed a heavily knuckled finger at the wall walks.

We all turned in the direction he pointed. Indeed, we saw several armored soldiers standing or pacing along the walks between the castle's many towers, but their feet seemed heavy and I saw no fight in their gait.

George was fingering the amulet beneath the cloth of his tunic as he squinted at the face of the gatekeeper.

"Was your head crushed in battle?" he asked. Sir Andrew frowned at George's impulsiveness.

The old man laughed. "Indeed it was, my boy. Did you think my old mum dropped me on my head when I was a babe?" he asked, swiping at George's head with his big pawed hand.

Sir Andrew's frown lengthened. He pulled at his tunic impatiently. "Are you not going to lead the princess to her residence? It has been an exhausting journey and I am anxious to see her safe in her quarters."

The gatekeeper straightened as if insulted. "Indeed I am. The mayor is waiting for you there." Turning quickly on his one good leg, he called over his shoulder, "Come along."

The back of my neck was tingling as we followed the

old man to the keep, the largest tower of the castle that held the king's residence and arsenal. He went through the doorway first, and we followed in single file. Sir Andrew and I were sandwiched between the soldiers as we climbed up the narrow stone stairway. I allowed my one hand to slide along the comforting coolness of the stone walls, while I used my other hand to ensure that George was behind me.

I knew we had reached the princess's residence when I smelled the fire and saw the flickering torchlight casting shadows over the top of the stairs.

"Sir Andrew!" a voice called. Sir Andrew was suddenly embraced by a fit man in a gray tunic and red surcoat despite the warmth of August. The dark-haired man clung to Sir Andrew, as if filled with emotion or exhaustion. It was hard to tell which. When they parted, I observed the man's deep-set brown eyes. The pleasure of this reunion was absent from them. His beard and temples were streaked with white. The lot of us were crowded on the floor now, staring at Sir Andrew and the gentleman.

"That fool of a gatekeeper was to summon me as soon as you arrived," he coughed weakly and shook his head. "I cannot afford to be strict now, under the circumstances."

Sir Andrew stepped back as the gentleman bowed at me.

"Forgive me, Princess Joan. Sir Andrew and I have fought together in numerous battles." His darkened eyes suddenly looked bright. "He saved my life not that long ago."

I nodded and smiled serenely, as the princess had shown me. She had thought it best that I never speak while playing her part.

"This is mayor Raymond de Bisquale, princess," Sir Andrew interceded, looking warmly at his friend. George was staring at Sir Andrew with his mouth open. I knew he had never thought of the red-faced Sir Andrew in a heroic light.

The mayor reached out suddenly and grasped Sir Andrew's hand. "We must talk, Andrew, but first we should allow the princess to rest." He gestured for me to sit on a velvet-cushioned chair. A small fire smoldered in the middle of the room. The hanging tapestries, darkened with soot, had witnessed many such fires. "I will see that refreshments are brought up immediately," he offered as he bowed again before heading to the stairs.

I walked over to the fire but remained standing. I watched as the mayor leaned into Sir Andrew's shoulder and spoke close to his ear. Our soldiers were lined along the wall, shifting nervously beneath the weight of their armor. Henry stood closest to the two gentlemen. I could see by his eyes that he could hear what they were saying.

"Nell," George whispered. "Why isn't the mayor happy to see the princess? Isn't her wedding supposed to be a happy occasion?"

Before I could reply, Henry approached as Sir Andrew seemed to decide to follow the mayor down the stairway.

"I can tell you why, boy," he said, but he looked at me as he spoke. I glanced at the other soldiers to see if they were curious as to why Henry addressed me, but they were peering out the windows and loopholes of the room. They were far more curious about the lack of activity at the castle.

"Henry, you really must be careful," I said. "You can never approach me when I am playing the princess."

"I know that," he replied impatiently. "But this is important. Do you want to know what the mayor whispered to Sir Andrew or not?"

My heart seemed to pause. "Of course," I said. "What is wrong here?"

"It's the pestilence," he said, the irritation completely gone from his voice. "The king's own plague has paid no regard to the ocean that separates England from Bordeaux." George grabbed my skirt as he said it and I couldn't help but let out a gasp. For the first time, I recognized the eyes of that long-ago gravedigger in Henry's face.

The Black Prince would have none of it. Despite the appeals of Sir Robert, Sir Andrew, and the mayor, who walked as if he were carrying death on his back, escorting the princess back to our ship and home was out of the question.

I hadn't meant to eavesdrop, but from our loft over the princess's quarters, I could hear the prince berate the king's advisors for suggesting that we flee to the safety of England.

"We are about to pledge the promise of a marriage that will ensure England's reign as the most powerful empire in the world. Would you have me turn my back on such an opportunity for my king?" the Black Prince hissed.

"I just don't believe your father would gamble the fate of such a deal against the pestilence. The marriage can be postponed some weeks." Sir Robert sounded severe.

"Coward. I don't know why my father surrounds himself with you timid dogs." I could imagine the prince's face pinched in contempt.

"My lord, if I can beg your understanding." Sir Andrew's voice choked with emotion. "Sir Robert fears for your life and that of the princess. He lost his entire family during the last pestilence."

"The princess will be fine," the Black Prince insisted. "I will watch over her."

During those somber days in the castle, I tried to keep George from peering out the window of our loft to watch the black smoke rise from the burning houses in the town. Houses marked with the cross of this plague. Despite his age, I knew he remembered as clearly as I the choking fear that gripped us as we watched our parents slowly die. Their delirium was infectious, and I felt anew the horror of running through London alleyways as I begged for someone to save my parents. The people I found in the streets screamed at me and ran the other way, seeing only the pestilence on my clothes. On my person. I had returned home to find George with a stick in his hand, waving it at a black rat he had cornered. "He was bothering Mum," he said, his eyes bright with the terror that was missing from his voice.

We trembled as we stood now on the wall walks, empty except for a soldier or two with the same fear of the pestilence in their eyes. Deserting the castle would mean death, as they would be traitors of the king. And only this new plague awaited them beyond the castle's walls. They, too, saw the piles of clothes, food, and furniture that were burning on the beaches. I wondered if the remaining soldiers noticed the rats scampering from one smoldering pile to the next.

One night I was sure that I saw the prince on the beach. He was dressed in black, carrying a cloth sack thrown over his shoulder. In one hand, he held the horn of a unicorn, the horn he blew to summon his men to battle, but what battle was he preparing for on this beach? I stood on the wall walk, shivering in the light gown I used for sleeping. A haze surrounded the moon. A haze created by the burning of Bordeaux.

I had leaned over the wall, mesmerized by the long, frantic shadow cast by the prince as he lurked around the pyres. The beach was deserted due to the hour, allowing the prince to skulk around the fires unimpeded. *What is he looking for?* I wondered as I watched him drop to his knees to lunge at something unseen. He appeared to struggle with something before he shoved it into his bag. I thought of the squeals that George heard behind the prince's closed door on the ship and a similar noise, multiplied many times, that I had heard coming from the keep's dungeon. Surely he was not collecting those creatures.

I didn't have much time to dwell on the prince's strange activities. For within three weeks of our arrival at the castle, Sir Robert, Father Paul, and the princess were dead.

imposter

THE RED VELVET of the princess's dress felt cool to the touch. How quickly it had lost her warmth, I thought, as I folded the dress to pack it neatly in one of the many bridal trunks brought along for the wedding. Sir Andrew had asked me to stay in the princess's quarters to ensure that her possessions were in order before the trunks were returned to the ship. He said that the king was meticulous about such matters. Anything missing would have been defilement, for only the king could order the burning of the princess's clothes. Did it matter, as the castle air was already tainted by the smoke from the smoldering possessions of the stricken villagers?

I took my time with each garment. I wanted to linger over every reminder of her—from the look on her

face of delighted astonishment on the day of our intro-
duction to our twilight whisperings about our twinned
future as we kept company belowdecks on our journey
to Bordeaux. The princess had become my life and my
sister when we were away from the world's eyes. What
would the princess's death mean for George and me?
Would the king still want me in his service or would I
appear to him like a ghost in his own castle? Just the sight
of me might drive him mad with grief. My stomach felt
knotted with fear.

George was sitting cross-legged on the stone floor,
fingering his amulet. His back was to the room's entrance.
His gaze roamed moodily from the princess's bed to her
dining table, to the unicorn tapestry that hung on the far
wall, until it settled on me. He no longer tried to hide
his amulet and instead wore it boldly over his tunic.
Under normal circumstances, I would insist that he hide
it. I didn't like George bringing attention to us. I wasn't
sure that it mattered here, in this place of death. The
amulet seemed to comfort him.

Despite the light tunic I was wearing, I was sweating
from the September warmth. George squinted at me,
inspecting my features for some sign of the pestilence.

"George, please stop staring at me. I don't have a

fever, it is only the heat," I said peevishly as I closed the lid to the last trunk. Ten of them lined the various walls of the room.

"Did these all belong to the princess?" he asked, amazed. "You and I, Nell, can collect all of our things in a sack," he added distractedly. "Why does a princess need so many clothes?"

I knew he didn't mean to bother me, but I was all cried out and all that was left in me at the moment was a simmering anger.

"Because she is a princess!" I yelled. "She represents the king and her country. How could you ask such a stupid question?"

The shouting made me feel better, even though my knees were shaking and I had to place my hand on the rough lid of one of the trunks to keep steady. George had lost all color in his face.

"Are we going to die, Nell, like Mother and Father?" he asked, before he dropped his head to sob.

The sound pierced my heart. I ran to him. "No, no, dear George. Forgive me," I cried as I squatted on the floor beside him and took his slight little body in my arms. "I don't mean to be cross with you. I am just sorry for the princess," I whispered into his hair. "We survived the king's plague before, and we will beat it again, I'm sure." I prayed my voice carried the confidence I lacked.

He wiped his eyes with a dirty hand, leaving a muddy streak.

"What is going to happen to us, Nell? I'm not sure that we can trust this amulet. It didn't protect the princess." He was peering at it closely, as if looking for any changes in its color or its image. The likeness of a rat was still all too clear.

I licked my thumb and wiped the smudge from his face. "Sir Andrew says that we are to go home. We need to tell the king what has happened to the princess." I lowered my voice as I had difficulty speaking of her. "The king will take care of us. We are a part of his household."

"Plans have changed, Nell," a voice corrected me from the other side of the room. The Black Prince filled the entranceway.

"M-my lord," I stammered as George and I scrambled to stand. I smoothed my hair and my dusty tunic with my hands. "I have finished preparing the princess's things for our journey home." I said this deliberately. Perhaps the prince was confused.

I kept my eyes on the pointy ends of his boots as he approached. They reminded me of tails.

Too soon, he stood directly in front of me. I could feel his hot breath on my face.

"Tell the brat to go," he said. He looked at me over the sharp edge of his nose.

George's head snapped up. "I need to stay with Nell to protect her."

The prince's smile twitched. "Protect her? From what? From me?" he asked. His voice was suddenly friendly.

"No, my lord." George shook his head vehemently. "From the pestilence. She needs to be near my amulet." He presented it to the prince. It filled the bowl of George's hand.

The prince bent to stare at it. He released a tiny sound of surprise. "Well, George. Your Nell will be doubly protected as I have one of those, too." Without hesitating, he pulled from his pocket an amulet and held it next to the one in George's hand. They were identical.

"Oh, my," George said. "Do you know John Moore, my blacksmith friend? Did he make this for you?"

"Indeed I do. It appears we both possess the power of the rat." He closed George's hand around the amulet. The prince's fingernails were long and sharp. "Now that you know that your sister is protected, I need to speak with her alone."

"Go ahead, George," I urged against the pounding of my heart. "See if your friend the gatekeeper needs something to eat. It's nearly midday and I don't think he has had relief." George had befriended the gatekeeper. The gatekeeper's misshapen head fascinated him and his comfortable banter eased George's heart.

George nodded. "I will be back soon, my lord, so that you are not inconvenienced in having to protect Nell." George did a quick bow and ran toward the stairway.

"What a remarkable boy," said the prince. The smile on his face was absent of all kindness. He scurried along the row of trunks, stopping here and there to lift a lid and inspect a garment. He allowed the last lid to close with a bang. The sound was harsh against the castle's stark walls.

"Sir Andrew will be along anytime now. He was eager to board the princess's things," I announced, anxious to interrupt the prince's survey. Although my heart was thudding against my ribs, I was also aware of a traitorous malice I felt toward the prince. *How dare he touch his sister's possessions with such disregard?* Surely he did not love her.

"Watch your pretty little face, Nell. My sister never looked at me like that." He smiled as I blushed, hot from my shame. "I want you to take off that rag you are wearing and replace it with one of my sister's dresses." He was resting his weight against the trunk by the door. "You are the princess now," he drawled.

I stood there numb, not comprehending what he was saying. He flicked his long black hair over his shoulder as he laughed.

"I—I don't know what you mean," I stammered.

"Surely you do," he objected as he rose to approach me. I closed my eyes as I felt his warmth suddenly inches from my body. I tried not to cringe as he twirled a strand of my hair on his finger.

"You are just as beautiful as the princess. The poor Prince Pedro will not have a clue that he has been duped. You will save this marriage for my father—our king," he hissed into my ear.

I stepped back and, without thinking, pushed his hand away. "It's not right! I cannot pretend to be the princess," I cried. The protest sounded feeble to my ears, yet I felt it with all my heart.

"Not right?" He laughed. His eyes seemed to shrink to mocking slits. "I tell you what is right and what is wrong. You dare to be so impudent in my presence?"

I shook my head. There was more to my objection.

"People will know I am not the princess," I insisted. "I don't know how to behave. What do I know about—"

"Living in splendor? In the arms of luxury?" The prince's face was only inches from my own. "You will never have to worry about your next supper or where you are going to sleep or whether your little brat will live to see his manhood." His dark eyes were wide now.

"I cannot pretend to be the princess forever," I persisted, despite the weakness in my muscles.

He grabbed my wrist, his nails digging into my skin. "Let me help you change your mind!" he shouted as he dragged me to the entranceway. I stumbled as I clawed at whatever I could to slow us down—a table that fell over or a chair that screeched as I dragged it across the floor. This only made him all the more impatient.

"Please!" I cried. "Where are we going?" I knew it was futile to beseech him, for now he had his back to me. The prince was hauling me across the floor and down the keep's winding stairway as if I were a troublesome dog. I thought about crying out as we passed the windows, but I saw no one in the courtyard. Besides, what soldier would come to my rescue? I only prayed that George would not see us.

He was mumbling to himself as we scrambled to the bottom floor. This room contained the castle's arsenal, and we were surrounded by armor, crossbows, swords, and lances that hung along the walls. I wondered if he might behead me as he threw me to the ground.

"How much do you care for your little brat, Nell?" he asked as he stood over me, shaking.

I could not answer him, as he had asked me the question that I feared more than any in the world. I hated myself for it, but I began to cry.

"Let me show you something, Nell," he murmured, stooping to kneel beside me to grab the handle of the trapdoor that was only inches from where I lay. The dungeon was below us.

The first thing I noticed as he slowly pulled at the wooden door was the terrible smell—the scent of creatures hungry and scared. In the blackness below, I could not see them, but I could hear their squeals. There must have been thousands of them piled on top of one another, clawing to get to the light.

"You are looking at me with that appalling expression again, my dear Nell. That will not do." The chilling, playful tone had returned to his voice.

"George likes rats, unlike you, Nell. Am I correct?" he asked, suddenly sitting cross-legged beside me, just as George had been doing when the prince had entered the princess's quarters. "I would be glad to show the brat my collection."

It would have been better for me if he had thrust a dagger through my heart. When the pestilence had taken my parents, I had vowed to protect George with my own life. By fate, I had been able to provide for him beyond all prayer. I had also exposed him to danger by vowing to protect the princess. The Black Prince had not played a part in my nightmares. What he was threatening to do now paled any horror I could imagine.

"All right," I said, cold to my bones. "I will be the princess."

That night, as we sat on our straw pallets beside the princess's empty bed, George and I made a pact. A single candle threw our conspiring shadows against the wall. They appeared as monstrous as the prince's afternoon visit.

I told him about the prince's plans—his desire to pass me off to the prince of Castile as the princess. I neglected to share the part in which he had threatened to feed George to the rats.

"But why is he doing this, Nell?" George cocked his head. The amulet rested in his lap.

"Because he believes that this is best for England." I said nothing about my own belief that the prince had his own selfish plans at heart.

"I don't agree with this, George," I said as I leaned

over and took George's hand. "I cannot pretend to be the princess. It would say that her life . . . and her death . . . were meaningless."

"Yours, too, Nell," he pointed out.

I turned my face away from him. Our lives had *value*, but only as long as we served the needs of the prince. The king was appointed by God to rule England. He, his family, and lords like Sir Andrew and Sir Robert were important, as what they did could change the lives of everyone. The poor—like George and me—were every-where. Our absence would not cause a ripple. I didn't want George to see my tears, so I rubbed my eyes as if I were tired.

"As soon as we get the chance, George, we must run away." I tried to sound calm, as if the act I was suggesting was a childish lark instead of treason.

George's eyes were wide with fear. He considered what I said and then nodded solemnly. A soft breeze from the window seemed to tickle George's dirty blond hair. Our shadows shimmered on the wall, knocking against the wooden posts of the princess's bed.

"What will be our signal?" he whispered.

I smiled, slightly reassured at George's knowledge of scheming.

"Hmmm." I paused. "I don't think we can plan a signal. It will have to be when we're alone." Either way, I thought, the prince would surely hunt us down. Better that we get a head start and scurry away from him.

When Sir Andrew entered the princess's quarters the next morning, his mouth worked as if to say something to me but nothing came out. He was dressed in a short black tunic with black stockings and slippers. His purse hung from his belt. As the king's emissary, Sir Andrew kept the king's seal there, in addition to the key to the chest that contained the king's gold. The morning sun was at his back as it streamed through the keep's windows. His white hair appeared like the texture of clouds.

He coughed, waiting for an explanation.

I was wearing one of the princess's favorite summer dresses, as the morning was already damp from the heat. It was a red-and-blue silk gown with golden Plantagenet lions sewn on both the skirt and blouse. I had found it laid out on the princess's bed when I awoke, along with her brush and looking glass. Apparently, the prince could move like a thief.

"Good morning, Sir Andrew." I curtsied. "Did you sleep well?" I was unsure of how to explain my garment. My face was red and I looked away to gain my composure.

"Nell." Sir Andrew's tone was sharp. "You are done with this playacting." He took a few hesitant steps into the room. He looked as if he were seeing a ghost.

I nodded in agreement. I knew this was wrong. Every nerve in my body ached at this betrayal of the princess. "You must help me," I began, but froze as I saw the form of the Black Prince fill the entranceway.

"How may I offer assistance, princess?" the prince purred as he did a quick bow. "May I braid your hair? The princess claims that I have a special gentleness," he explained to Sir Andrew.

He picked up the princess's brush and looking glass. He paused to smile at his reflection before he raised the brush to my head. My scalp prickled as if he held a weapon.

Sir Andrew's mouth was wide open now. His hand went to his heart. "My lord, what is the meaning of this? We are due to return to the ships today. The king will not look kindly on Nell's behavior." I could see a fine sheen of sweat appearing on Sir Andrew's forehead, upper lip, and nose. He looked as if he was sick.

The prince dropped the looking glass onto the bed and stroked his pointy black beard as he stared at Sir Andrew with contempt. "We are leaving for Spain this afternoon, dear Andrew. I have already spoken with the mayor about arranging for our horses. Thanks to this plague, he tells me he will have no problem with acquiring at least fifty of them."

"I don't understand," Sir Andrew replied—although his lifeless tone indicated he did.

The prince turned his attention back to my hair. His fingers were nimble as he began a braid. I stood like a statue.

"The princess has a betrothal to honor, my dear Sir Andrew. She intends to honor it and I intend to ensure that she arrives safely into Prince Pedro's arms." He was speaking to Sir Andrew as if to a child.

Sir Andrew was trembling. "But, my lord, this is impossible." His speech poured from him with agony, like blood from a wound. "I do not think the king would agree to this. What if Prince Pedro finds out? It could mean war!"

The prince's hand tightened around my braid. It took all my self-control to stop myself from crying out and reaching for his hands. "Pedro will know nothing. He doesn't speak English or French. He's a barbarian."

"But our soldiers know! And the mayor..." Sir Andrew stopped. I could imagine the prince's strangling gaze by the ferocity by which he held my hair.

"Those soldiers you worry over are *my* soldiers, dear Andrew. Each breath they dare take depends on my allowing them to breathe." The prince's hand was shaking. I prayed that Sir Andrew would not test his humor further.

"You, Sir Andrew, will ensure the mayor's allegiance. Otherwise you may lose one more dear friend."

Sir Andrew turned away. His hands were fists.

But Sir Andrew had said something that stopped my heart. War. I hadn't thought about my failure as the princess's imposter reaching such a disastrous scale.

"I can finish my hair, my lord." I pulled away from him. I wanted him to listen to Sir Andrew.

The prince arched his dark eyebrows mockingly. "See that, Andrew? She is already acting just like a princess."

"Nell!" George's yell preceded him as he raced up the keep's stairway. He ran into the room, out of breath, as he stood with a pewter bowl full of meat and white bread.

"She eats like a princess, too," the prince finished triumphantly.

"But she's not the princess," George protested. "Anyone can see that she is Nell."

"Precisely," Sir Andrew dared to whisper as he placed his hand on George's shoulder.

The prince tossed the brush onto the bed. "You bore me, Andrew." He smiled, but his voice was thick with threat.

"Come here, George," the prince said darkly as he stooped until his eyes were level with George's. George held the bowl of food against his chest. "We not only share amulets that will protect us against the pestilence but we also share a sister."

George bit his lip as the prince breathed into his face. "We shall call her Princess Joan now."

George took a few steps back, never taking his gaze from the prince's angular face.

The prince straightened and turned to me. "Be ready to leave when the sun hits its height, princess. And you, Andrew," he mocked as he swaggered toward him, indicating with a flip of his hand for Sir Andrew to step aside. "You can do what you wish."

We listened to his footsteps as he descended the stairs, until the silence of the castle swallowed all sound and we were left with only the deafening beats of our hearts.

black heart

THE NOISE OF BUSY SOLDIERS and the smell of saddled horses filled the courtyard. As the Black Prince promised, the beasts were lined along the castle's crenellated walls, facing the keep. They whinnied and stamped their hooves nervously as the soldiers, some already in their riding armor, prepared for our journey. The sun was high and hot. I squinted, but otherwise did my best to appear regal as I scanned the soldiers for the prince and Sir Andrew.

I found the prince standing with the gatekeeper, the reins of his enormous black stallion in his royal owner's hands. His horse, like the others, was draped in the yellow-and-red heraldic coat of arms of the Plantagenets. I looked down at my skirt and the lions that marked me, as much as the horses, as a possession of the king.

The prince was already in his full battle armor—black as the color of his horse. I wondered if perhaps the prince did not feel the heat, if he truly was beyond human frailties. A sword hung from his leather belt, and the chain mail from his helmet hid his beard and neck so that his thin face appeared incredibly small. He was in an animated conversation with the gatekeeper and pointing with his gauntlet toward me as he grabbed the gatekeeper's tunic and shook him. The poor man's dented head wobbled violently on his shoulders. He pushed away from the prince, dropped to his knees, and bowed his head in compliance.

"What is the prince doing to the gatekeeper?" George asked, his voice rising with concern for his new friend. He stood a few paces behind me since he was no longer allowed to stand beside me in public.

The soldiers standing nearest to us glanced nervously at me. Their weary stares told me to quiet George.

"The prince is merely giving the gatekeeper his instructions, George," I announced, doing my best to mimic the princess's confident tone. I didn't dare turn to address him. I had warned him not to approach me, but I did tell him never to let me out of his sight, for I could not predict the best moment for our escape. I knew we would have to decide in a heartbeat.

Thankfully, Sir Andrew suddenly appeared by my side.

"We are almost ready to depart, princess," he said. His voice was tired and flat. We stood silently together for a moment, as we both surveyed the scene before us.

"Sir Andrew, is this everyone? We had a hundred soldiers when we left our ships," I noted.

"This is what remains of their number, princess," he replied. "The pestilence has taken twenty of them already, and another fifteen are too ill to travel."

"Is Henry all right?" I asked. I hadn't seen him since the day we learned about the pestilence. My heart seemed to pause when I asked the question.

Sir Andrew turned to look at me. His bushy white eyebrows arched as he gave me a sad smile. "The young soldier is fine, princess. The prince sent him into the village a few days ago to assist with the collection of provisions for our journey. He and the other soldiers will meet up with us in town."

Despite the heat, I was trembling. We were ready to leave for Spain and begin this two-week journey that would deliver me to Prince Pedro, if we all did not die from the pestilence first. Which fate would be worse for

George and me? And which fate would be worse for England should Prince Pedro recognize me for the imposter that I am?

The prince had woven a plausible tale to blot out my identity. Last night he had summoned us all into the courtyard—Sir Andrew, the mayor, the gatekeeper, and our soldiers. The near full moon was at his back as it reflected a ghostly glow upon the faces of his subjects while shadowing the prince's face. He wore a black hooded cloak against the late summer evening chill. It billowed in the breeze as he made his announcement.

"The princess has asked me to share the somber news of Nell's death from the cursed plague." He pursed his lips in a convincing display of sorrow. "As you can imagine, the princess has been silenced momentarily by her devastating grief, as Nell was a loyal servant whom the princess treated like a sister." The prince glanced at me and hung his head, as if overcome on my behalf.

"My task is to protect the princess from the pestilence and so we are leaving tomorrow for Castile—to ensure that the princess makes it safely to her betrothed." I felt my face flush with shame as I noticed that no one dared glance at me, for they knew that it was the real princess who was dead. "Before we depart to our own quarters, I

ask that you all beseech our lord as Nell's vanquished
body burns upon the beach pyre to keep the rest of us
safe, just as Nell would have wanted it," he said almost
wistfully, turning to cast a smile at me with an intensity
that knotted my gut.

I heard George behind me, making those odd sounds
that he did when he wished to speak but knew better.
The prince heard his muffled protests, too.

"Forgive me, George," the prince suddenly bellowed,
losing all trace of the false sincerity he practiced so well.
"You must be wondering about your own fate, now that
your loving sister has departed us." I held my breath, praying for George to remain silent. When he said nothing, the
prince bestowed a condescending smile as he continued.

"The young brat will remain with the princess," he
added, "as she was extremely fond of Nell. Is the princess
not a most generous woman?" he demanded of us, lifting
the sides of his cloak as if he had wings. The soldiers
snapped to attention as if signaled.

"Aye," the soldiers yelled back, banging their swords
against the ground until the courtyard was filled with the
deafening clamor.

The prince flashed me a knowing smile. He didn't
need the words to say what was in his heart. *Precious*

George is my dagger at your delicate throat, Nell. I will protect our George like a royal ransom. I flinched and turned away from him. Even the air between us was tainted by him.

"Ah, my dear sister," the Black Prince hissed, trotting to us on his horse. He was holding the reins of a white horse, which trailed behind his own. "You are beautiful," he said, leering. I straightened, struggling to meet his stare as if I were truly the princess. I knew by now that he relished the advantages of royalty. Perhaps in public at least I could thwart his bad treatment of George and me.

"You do know how to ride, do you not?" he asked, amused.

"I do, my lord," I replied.

"Then help her onto the horse, Sir Andrew," the prince commanded.

Sir Andrew bowed as he guided me gently by the elbow.

"Your Highness!" a voice called breathlessly from behind us. We all turned to see the mayor hurrying from the keep. He walked with the stride of the proud, yet his face seemed carved with new lines and the white at his temples combed more of his dark hair.

"Forgive me for delaying you," he apologized, bowing to the prince. "I would be a negligent host if I did not wish you a safe journey and a safe return."

The prince bestowed a tiny smile. "Thank you, Sir. I have given the gatekeeper his instructions. I will leave it to you to see that they are carried out."

"You can be sure of that, my grace." The mayor bowed. He then turned to Andrew and placed a heavy hand on Andrew's shoulder. "Until we meet again, Andrew." The mayor's brown eyes were full as he stared into the face of his friend. He then turned to me and dropped to one knee.

"Princess, may God protect you and bless your marriage," he said loudly, as if he wished the entire army to hear. I drew in my breath as if slapped by the force of his delivery. It felt unnatural and I realized that the mayor and I and all surrounding us were playacting in some ghastly drama. Our band of soldiers was frozen atop their horses. George stood a few yards behind the mayor, holding his breath. The amulet hung from his neck and George was holding it in his right hand. Sir Andrew was statuelike beside the mayor, with closed eyes and lips pulled taut. The prince was looking down at us all, only the muscles in his face twitched.

The mayor pressed his lips to the back of my left hand. As he did, I felt something delicate, like a fallen leaf, slip into my palm. A second before he stood again, he looked into my eyes with a tiny glimmer of hope.

"Let's go!" the prince yelled, breaking the stillness.

I was afraid to unclasp my hand as I held the reins of my horse. The small piece of parchment that it guarded throbbed in my fist. The princess had taught me to read. Together, we had struggled to understand the Bible verses, so carefully copied by the monks. As the king was selected by God, he insisted that his children become familiar with his stories. "Invoke God's words in all that you do, and you will never be conquered," he had told the princess. I never saw such threat in the Bible's words.

Still I worried. I had never been tested by a letter or message. I prayed that the words would be familiar to me. I did not dare look at it now or try to hide it in my dress for fear that the prince would see me.

We were riding in pairs as we entered the town of Bordeaux. The great castle loomed on the mountain behind us now, blocking out all view of the sea. The sun beat upon our shoulders, but none of us complained as we wiped our damp foreheads. The prince rode a few paces in front of me. Sir Andrew, who shared his horse with George, rode beside me. Despite himself, George was smiling, as we had never ridden such magnificent beasts. We were usually relegated the oldest mares among

the king's stallions. I could not help but look with suspicion toward Sir Andrew. *Why is he keeping George so close
to him? Is he following the prince's orders?*

We smelled the village before we entered it. The air
was stained with smoke and the smoldering odors of
wood, clothes, and flesh. I wondered if they had gathered
all the cats and dogs in Bordeaux for the cleansing, as they
had done in London all those years ago.

The prince raised his hand to signal stop as we
approached the village's entrance. The soldiers behind him
called to the soldiers in front of us. They turned, pulling
the reins of their horses to allow the prince, in his full
battle regalia, to enter the town first. It was said that the
Black Prince feared nothing and that his black armor
paused even the bravest hearts. His pleasure of being the
first in a column of soldiers to ride into a city dressed as
England's warrior showed off a confidence meant to pique
the fear of his enemies. An army that allows its leader on
the first line is an army that does not know defeat.

He had been fighting in France for years now and
seemed self-assured as he used his horse to push aside his
mounted captain. I was familiar with the bitter complaints
of the soldiers when we were still at Windsor. It was said
that at the slightest sign of aggression, soldiers nearest the

prince were counted upon to throw themselves in front of him. The prince could not be expected to take the arrows of the enemy. The soldiers hated this spectacle.

As we waited for the soldiers to realign behind the prince, I wondered if I should steal a peek at the tiny piece of paper that the mayor had pressed into my hand. The prince was preoccupied, as were the soldiers nearest him. I looked beside me to Sir Andrew, who was frowning at the exercise in front of us. George kept his face forward, appearing mesmerized by the prince, but when he felt my stare upon him, he brushed it away with his hand. I knew that if our gazes met, he would want to share his excitement. I felt the warmth of pride although I ached to be simply his sister again.

It was then that I noticed that as soon as I caught the eye of a soldier, he would quickly look away. *They are only following orders, I reminded myself, just as I am. Nell is dead to them*, I thought as I caught a rising sob in my throat. I slowly looked down into my opening palm.

"Forward!" the captain yelled as our horses suddenly lurched with the order. My fist closed tightly around the reins. We entered the village.

At first I could only hear the sound of hooves on the narrow cobblestone road that led us into the maze of

Bordeaux. Rickety wooden homes and stores lined each street gutter, their second stories leaning perilously close to their neighbors. The roofs blocked out the hot sun and the streets were pitched in shadow. At first we did not see many people—a furtive head behind a window shutter, a gnarled hand closing a door. The reason was all too apparent. Almost every door had been slashed with the cross of this plague, including the doors we passed of the apothecary, the blacksmith, the shoemaker, and the grocer.

As we wound our way along the cobble streets, the captain would yell, "Make way for the prince!" The Black Prince held his head and shield high before him, but there was no one to make way. The houses we passed still smoldered, and those that were not burning seemed starkly quiet. Only the black rats that darted boldly across our path or paused in the shadows of opened doorways attested that Bordeaux still held some life.

I glanced at George, who gripped Sir Andrew's belt as he squeezed his eyes closed. I wanted to hold him, for I knew he was witnessing the death of our parents all over again—just as I was. I prayed that George's amulet would protect us.

Finally we reached the village square. A fountain, still bubbling, lay in its center. Behind the fountain was a great stone church whose spire seemed to pierce the blue sky. There were people at the church who stood behind its black iron fence. They said nothing as the prince signaled us forward again, around the fountain, until we congregated in front of the church's red doors.

I took a deep breath. There were probably fifty or so men, women, and children. They all looked the same as they grasped the iron bars of the fence, staring at us with the sunken eyes of despair. Their clothes and hair were dirty. Their children leaned lifelessly against their knees. *How many towns would meet their end like this*, I wondered, *just as they had in England years ago?* I thought of the priest in Portsmouth who warned us that death lay waiting in our future. *How did he know?*

Although his back was to me, I noticed that the prince was shaking. *Is he overcome at the plight of these people?* The expressions of the soldiers surrounding me told me that they believed they were looking at death.

Suddenly the Black Prince roared as he leaped from his horse. The soldiers closest to him dismounted.

"Do you maggots know who you are staring at?" he cried, flashing his sword. "I am your lord!"

I looked at him in disbelief. He had fought many battles to gain the French territories. It riled him that his new subjects did not recognize him, or that if they did, they were too close to death to care.

"Please, my lord," Sir Andrew interrupted, directing his horse forward. George still clung to his belt. "These people, *your* people, have lived through the pestilence, and death is at their own doors."

The prince flashed him a look. The hairs on the back of my neck stood when the prince bared his teeth at Sir Andrew as he cracked his sword against the pavement. The people barely flinched. "Where is the priest?" he seethed.

For a moment, nobody answered, as our little army faced off with the already defeated villagers living in the church's graveyard.

"He's dead," a man closest to the church's door finally offered. He said it without emotion. "As we all soon will be."

My throat tightened as I searched the faces of the children. The fire of their lives had been suffocated and their spirits had burned out. If the pestilence did not kill them, starvation would. My own plague wounds caused my eyes to blaze angrily. These children could have been George and me in London years ago. Their parents could have been my mother and father.

"We must save them!" I burst out. All heads snapped in my direction. Sir Andrew looked appalled and George was wide-eyed. The prince tapped the edge of his sword in his gloved hand. He was smiling at me, but the smile was deadly.

"Indeed, princess. And how do you suggest that we do that?" he challenged. His voice was incredibly calm. "Shall we take them all with us as your own little ragamuffin bridal party?"

"My lord!" a voice yelled from the square. It was Henry and a few of the soldiers who had been sent into the village to collect our provisions. Henry came forward on his horse, glancing at me nervously and then back to the prince.

"My lord," he repeated as he bowed his head. "We were extremely fortunate in our collections. We found smoked chickens and duck at the butchers, salted fish at the fishmonger's, and baskets of vegetables at the market, most of them still good." He paused to catch his breath. "Also, it appears that the village had an early harvest of barley and rye, before the pestilence struck, I presume."

The prince cocked his head. "Then why are these people starving behind these gates, like caged animals?" he asked.

"Because they are afraid to venture where this plague may still lurk," I thought I whispered, but again saw faces, if not their gazes, looking in my direction. "Let us leave them some of the food," I suggested in my best princess voice, although my heart went cold when the prince narrowed his eyes.

"We do have more than enough," Henry confirmed, not looking at me but addressing the prince.

The prince smiled and kicked at a stone. He slid his sword back into its sheath. "As the princess wishes," he ordered. "Let us get out of this horrid village."

We rode for hours until dark, until the smell of Bordeaux no longer tortured our noses with its infected smoke. That was one small relief, for as long as I could detect the burning scent, my mind would not release the haunted faces of the children in the church graveyard. I looked at George as we neared a small farming village. He was barely awake and his blond head leaned into Sir Andrew's wide back as he swayed in rhythm with the horse. I was tired, too, yet that the prince had peeled off his battle armor and was now wearing his hooded black cape did not escape my notice. *There must not be anyone worth impressing in this town*, I thought.

The sky was pink as we approached the first thatched

property. The sun was ready to kiss the horizon. Soon it would be snatched by the night and kept hostage until morning—like George and me. I remembered the parchment in my hand and squeezed it to reassure myself that it was still there. I worried that I must read it before all light was lost.

"The town looks whole," Sir Andrew muttered to no one in particular as our line of horses stopped to allow a few of the soldiers to select the best overnight residence for the prince. Except for the quiet, the little hamlet looked in order. Cows and goats grazed in the pasture that unfolded behind the wood-and-thatched-roofed homes that lined the dirt road. Fences looked well tended and smoke escaped from chimneys in little puffs. Some unseen roosters crowed and the sound cut my heart, foreshadowing the peacefulness that would not reign here again until the prince was gone.

"Well!" he yelled from his horse, obviously impatient. "What have you found?" Two soldiers who we had been watching hurried on their horses to the prince's side.

"The house on the end here is probably the most comfortable, my lord," the soldier said, nodding as if that would encourage the prince to better agree.

"Really?" the prince drawled as he played with the tip of his beard. His mouth was in a pout.

The second soldier, this one much younger than his partner, nodded more enthusiastically. "There is a good stock of food, my lord, in addition to a nice fire and some clean straw pallets. The owners were only honored to oblige," he added, wearing a stupid grin.

Suddenly the prince did the same as we all watched a man and woman with two small children scurry from their home. They headed to the wooden barn by the pasture with a few blankets in their hands.

"Well, as long as they don't mind the company of soldiers, we all will be fine," remarked the prince.

I frowned and wondered, *What kind of man finds pleasure in the suffering of others?*

"Princess!" the prince interrupted. "You have that perturbed look on your face again," he chided. "You and the boy will stay with me tonight."

My heart stopped. I opened my mouth to protest but knew I could not push the prince. I nodded as I dismounted and gave the reins to a soldier. Sir Andrew gently lowered George to the ground. I took his hand, forgetting my role momentarily, and followed the prince into the farmer's house.

I did not feel as guilty as I should have watching George eat the peasants' meal of warm stew. It was slowly bubbling in a pot on a fire in the middle of the room when we entered, the family's wooden bowls arranged expectantly on the table. George eagerly drank the stew, raising the bowl to his lips. I looked at his thin face as he smiled at me shyly. It was hard for him to get used to seeing me in the princess's clothes. The torchlight cast dark hollows under his eyes. I prayed it was only the torchlight.

The prince wiped his mouth with his sleeve. "Are you not going to eat?" he asked, scowling at me. "It would not do for the princess to get weak and ill," he warned.

"I've eaten a bit," I replied, although I felt as if I had already taken too much. "I hoped to leave some for the family," I said, looking at the prince on the other side of the table. Sir Andrew sat beside me, breaking a small brown loaf in his hands.

"My dear sister is sometimes like a nun, Andrew." The prince laughed as he reached for a piece of the bread. Sir Andrew continued to mop up the broth at the bottom of his bowl.

"Would you be so good as to clean up, my dear sister?" the prince asked. His tone was playful again as he handed me what was left of his dinner. He stood and grabbed the black cloak that he had hung on a hook by the door. "I will be back, my sweet. Don't wait up." He must have spied some relief in my face. "Our soldiers are on watch. No one can get in or leave this house while I am gone," he added.

"Andrew, come with me," he ordered, as if it were a second thought. Sir Andrew pulled himself up from the table with the jagged motions of an old man.

The prince was almost out the door when he turned to give us one last look.

"George," he said, pulling his amulet from his cloak pocket. "Is your amulet close to you?"

George sat straight up, suddenly wide-awake. "Why, yes, my lord. Here it is, around my neck," he said brightly as he held it between his fingers for the prince to see.

"Good, my boy. Keep it by my sister, who was so loved by your sister, while I am gone." He shot me a loaded smile. George nodded but crinkled his nose as if puzzled.

After the prince and Sir Andrew were gone, we sat at the table for a few more minutes, watching the shadow of the torchlight dance around the room. We allowed the stew fire to burn itself out. I listened to ensure that the prince was not lurking outside the door.

"George, could you take the remainder of the stew and bread to the family? I believe they are in the barn."

"Sure, Nell." He jumped up, eager to have a task. I did

not correct the use of my name but watched him as he carefully picked up the pot by its handle, using a rag that was hanging on the wall beside some kettles and cooking spoons. He held it with both hands as he pushed against the door with his back.

"I'll be right back," he promised.

As soon as he was out the door I opened my hand, eager to read the message buried in my palm. The crumpled paper was damp, and I prayed that the words it contained were still legible. I smoothed the paper on the surface of the table and peered at the single word in tiny black script.

G-R-A-C-I-A-S. I spelled out the word in my head and felt a rising sense of panic. *What does it mean?* I stood and paced around the embers of the fire, saying the letters aloud. I hoped that their sounds would blend into something that would tell me what to do.

"Nell?"

I jumped and turned to see George and Henry in the doorway. Henry had removed his riding armor and now wore a dust-covered brown tunic and stockings. Instead of spurs, pieces of hay clung to his ankles.

"Nell, are you okay? You're not sick, are you?" George asked. His eyes were wide as he clutched his amulet.

"Yes, I'm fine, dear," I replied, and knelt down to give him a hug. "But you must not call me Nell, not as long as I am doing the bidding of the prince. Do you understand?"

He frowned and bit his lip. Finally he nodded as I stared into his pale blue eyes. How I longed to be called Nell again.

I looked up to meet Henry's contemplative gaze.

"How are you, Princess?" he asked. There was just a tinge of sarcasm in his voice.

"I am well," I said as I tried to ignore my pounding heart and burning cheeks. I wanted to say so much, but I turned away from him, saying nothing.

"He followed me from the barn," George complained. "I told him that I could protect you."

"What are you going to do?" Henry asked. His hands rested on his hips, waiting impatiently for my answer. *What does he expect of me? Can I trust him?*

"I don't know," I replied. "He is our prince." I looked into Henry's eyes for some spark that would tell me that I could trust this young soldier, but he turned away and walked wordlessly out the door.

My heart sank. *We are truly on our own,* I thought as I dropped the piece of paper onto the glowing embers of the fire. George tugged at my hand but said nothing as we watched it curl up and disappear.

That night I dreamed of rats. Under the light of the moon, they moved as a single entity snaking down the road into the village. The sound of their march was deafening. They squealed and hissed with delight.

In my dream, George bolted from his pallet to use his amulet. "We must warn the prince!" he yelled.

"Don't bother, George. The prince already knows about the rats," I told him wearily. "See for yourself."

George and I opened the shutters and saw the prince in his hooded black cloak and his long pointy boots parading down the road, his sword in one hand and his lioncovered shield in the other. Behind him were his army of rats, their noses and whiskers twitching excitedly at the fresh scent of the village.

jester

A WEEK HAD PASSED SINCE we had left the farming
village and each day seemed to cast a longer,
darker shadow over our fate. I feared that I
would never find an opportunity to flee the prince.

At first I hoped that we might have the chance to get
lost in the throng of people who were traveling along the
coastal road. During the first few days, we passed hundreds
who had fled villages along the beaches—villages that the
pestilence had suddenly struck. The survivors headed
south, as did we, away from Bordeaux.

As the coastal road was narrow, our small army rode
side by side in twos or threes. We journeyed as if we were
initiating a small crusade. Passersby stepped off the road to
allow us to pass—the expressions on their faces were

either resentful or too world-weary to care. The soldiers, the horses, the clothes we wore and the trunks and other supplies we hauled, all reeked of our wealth. It felt blasphemous to me when we confronted faces disfigured by despair.

There were also those you expect to see on the highway—monks, nuns, pilgrims, beggars, and merchants—going about their business as if nothing else in the world mattered. We passed farmers who were herding their cows and sheep. Other families pulled their meager belongings in shared carts like mules. It was the families that left me feeling raw. What if we had left London when the last plague struck, as my mother had pleaded with my father? Would they still be alive? How simple and different our lives could have been.

During those first long days, I often felt as if I were being lulled into submission by the rigors of our journey. The prince insisted that we spent at least eight hours on our horses. Our only breaks were brief stops for eating the roasted rabbits and chickens acquired from the traveling merchants. At sundown we would stop to establish camp, for the prince was no longer interested in looking for an inn or a home that would host us as its guests. He was suddenly impatient to reach Castile. I assumed it was because he, too, feared the pestilence, but Sir Andrew mentioned another reason to me with a sour smile. "He doesn't want to lose a second sister, princess."

It was George who kept me focused during those long hours on the road. I feared that if we did not get away from the prince before we reached Castile, I might lose George forever. And despite the fate that awaited us at the end of our journey, I was cheered that George's heart had not hardened. During one of our breaks—consisting of cheese and bread since the prince did not want to waste the time of cooking over a fire—I was surprised to see George sharing his scanty meal with two little beggar girls, who had been running alongside our horses since we passed their village. The girls' dresses were tattered and dirty. They were shoeless and their hair was knotted. I guessed they might be all of six years old. George was dividing his bread and cheese among the three of them, patting the ground beside him to encourage them to sit. Suddenly, as I watched them, I panicked. *Will George become just like them?*

"Who are your little friends, George?"

The girls looked up, their eyes wide in their dirty faces.

"I don't know their names, my lord Prince, as I don't

speak French," he replied innocently. "But I know they are hungry," he added. "Did you want to share some of your cheese?"

For a moment, the prince simply stared, baffled by the question. My own heart stood still. He then smiled at the two little girls as if they were an interesting diversion.

"Why not, my dear George? I speak French, but I needn't waste my time asking them anything. I can see they are hungry." The prince crouched beside the girls as if he might poke them. They leaned away from him, clutching each other's arms. "This hard cheese does not particularly please my palate anyway," the prince remarked as he stood again, apparently bored already with the terrorized girls. He motioned to one of his soldiers to gather his leftovers.

"Do you have your amulet, George?" he asked then, turning back to George as if it were a second thought.

"Right beneath my shirt, my lord Prince." George smiled brightly, patting his chest at the spot the amulet pressed against his flesh.

"Good. Let your little friends touch it, to protect them on the road."

George nodded and began pulling at the string around his neck.

I felt a cold chill grip me as I thought about my dream and looked at the two little sisters who we would be leaving behind to the prince's army of rats. *It is only a dream*, I reminded myself.

By the time we marked our second week on the road, the horses had grown tired of the constant rise and fall of the rock-strewn paths, but the soldiers were patient with them, as everyone was hot and tired under the glare of the early October sun. I wore the same Plantagenet dress but no longer worried that it was dirty or stained from our journey. For with my dusty dress, I seemed to blend more naturally into the scenery. To be clean would have diminished the horrors we witnessed—horrors that the prince seemed to relish.

We passed many villages on the edge of abandonment or already deserted. It was easy to see that this plague was traveling down the coast. Homes stood like shells, the thatch of the roofs gone from the burnings and their wooden walls scorched. Black rats darted in and out of alleys, stopping to stare at us as we passed as if we were the intruders. All we saw were burning pyres on the beaches and more than one abandoned ship listing off the coastline. We heard the rumors that the mayor had burned all of Bordeaux, and even the castle was in flames.

Suddenly the steady stream of people had stopped, and I felt as if our little army was alone in this part of the world. It was then I began to despair.

The prince barely left me alone or out of his sight, and when he did he was sure to assign a few soldiers "to guard me from harm."

"It is dangerous in the woods, dear sister," he said slyly as he pulled his black brute alongside my horse. He would point into the particularly thick coppice of trees and brush that periodically flared on the inland side of the road as he leaned toward me. "Do you know who lives in there, my dear? Robbers, thieves, beggars, all ready to prey upon a foreign princess."

"I have not seen any of them," I replied brusquely. Desperation slowly eroded my attempts to maintain a regal demeanor, but the prince seemed to take pleasure in my barely veiled fear.

He sat up straight on his horse, a delighted smile pulling at his features until he looked demonic. "The Spanish prince believes his betrothed to be a dove. How easily we men are fooled by beauty."

I did not want to be the cause of his enjoyment. I turned away and stared longingly into the wet, dark woods. If only a band of thieves were desperate or crazy enough to attack us.

But it was not a band of thieves that stopped us in our tracks—a man dressed in a multicolored tunic with bells on his hood and sleeves approached us on a black horse, followed by two foreign soldiers.

"*Saludos*, my lord Majesty," he pronounced as he bowed musically in his saddle, his bells tinkling high notes like laughter.

George let out a loud "Oh, my." The stranger had a dark beard and bushy black eyebrows. His nose was almost as pointy as the Black Prince's.

"My name is Gracias and I welcome you on behalf of Prince Pedro. I am to entertain you on the remainder of your journey. *?Es esta bueno?*"

"Really," the prince drawled, staring at the minstrel. He raised his hand to signal his army to be still. "What did you say your name was?" he asked, this time with a tone of amusement.

"Gracias!" the minstrel shouted, shaking his head so that his bells made one continuous peal. "G-R-A-C-I-A-S, thank you!" He threw his head back as I caught his darting glance.

The mayor's note, I thought, but felt a stab of panic. *Is this our savior? The minstrel of a foreign prince?*

"How do I know that you are who you say you are?" the prince asked evenly, his hand sliding to the hilt of his sword.

"I can recite for you a poem about your king or sing for you a song *romántico*," the minstrel replied. The bells on his sleeve softly tinkled as he flicked the reins of his horse to get closer to the prince. The prince was smiling now as if he dared Gracias to come one step closer. Our soldiers had gathered around the prince, their own swords on the brink of being pulled from their scabbards. The two Spanish soldiers, their armor and hair covered in a layer of dirt from the road, scowled at our soldiers as they shook their heads warning them to stay back. I held my breath.

"I can present to you a sealed letter from the prince intended for the eyes of his beloved." He said the word with a mocking sweetness.

Sir Andrew suddenly appeared, using his shoulders to press gently against a horse's flank to open a path. "May I see the letter? I am the king's ambassador, Sir Andrew Ullford," he explained, holding out his hand expectantly. "I daresay that I will recognize the seal of Prince Pedro."

Gracias stared at Andrew. The start of a smile tugged at his lips. They were opposites, I realized, as the two respected the momentary silence between them. Sir Andrew's cloud

of white hair and bulbous red face looked absurd against
the dark sharpness of Gracias's features. Yet, for a moment,
I recognized a hint of affection in Gracias's eyes.

"Of course. *Perdóneme* my tardiness." Gracias bowed as
he pulled a tied parchment from his tunic. "But the letter
is meant for the pleasure of the *princesa*," Gracias reminded
Sir Andrew as he handed over the paper.

Sir Andrew untied the ribbon gently. "Of course. I am
just checking the seal, sir."

"You will give the letter to me," the prince corrected.
"As I am the princess's protector."

Sir Andrew had his back to the prince. He squinted at
the broken blob of melted red wax. "Indeed. You are a
member of Prince Pedro's castle. How kind of the prince
to send you ahead," Sir Andrew said agreeably.

"Let me see that." The prince extended his hand
impatiently and snatched the parchment from Sir Andrew,
barely able to hide his sneer. "Prince Pedro sounds like a
man in love," the prince finally noted, tucking the letter
into the pocket of his own tunic.

I felt as if the roots of my hair were on fire. All of this
talk about the prince's love reminded me that we were
destined to meet within a few days time. I knew that I
could not allow that to happen—that once Prince Pedro

spent any time with me—this ruse would be discovered. *The time for our escape is now.* I looked around for George and saw that he had climbed onto the horse he shared with Sir Andrew to get a better view. He seemed transfixed by the minstrel.

"Who wrote the English for him?" the prince asked, deadly serious.

"I had the honor, my lord," Gracias replied quickly. "And may I say that Prince Pedro has boasted to all of the princesa's beauty."

Sir Andrew seemed to visibly exhale.

The prince almost smiled kindly at the minstrel. "Ah, yes. She is like an angel and her beauty can be blinding." His gaze rested on my perspiring brow. "Unpack your horses, Gracias, and join us for the night. We must celebrate the near end of our journey."

Gracias's reply was the shrill peal of his bells as he jumped from his saddle. He cast a last fleeting glance my way before he guided his horse to the clearing, where a few of the soldiers were already preparing our supper's fire.

That night, we sat around the popping kindling of the fire, privy to much entertainment and drink. Gracias and his soldiers were busy retrieving leather flagons full of

Iberia's finest madeiras from their horses' saddles. It appeared that they had carried nothing else with them on their journey from Castile.

"A welcome *feliz!*" Gracias shouted, "from Príncipe Pedro to his new *hermanos!*" He raised a flask and then passed it around before he launched into his own entertainment. The Black Prince leaned languidly against a log, his eyes small and contemplative as he surveyed the scene around him. As our soldiers drank, Gracias juggled three red balls in the air and caught them as if each were a small orb of fire. George was thrilled by the show. The blaze cast a feverish light to his pale face.

Gracias seemed never to tire as he laid aside his balls to dance or to sing some silly songs. His gaze encompassed every soldier at our camp, mentally tallying how many soldiers began to stumble over their own feet as the evening lengthened. His slippery stare landed upon me numerous times, but whenever I looked up from my own log to check his impropriety, his attention was back to the prince, who continued to watch his show with veiled contempt. The prince did not stop himself from enjoying the wine nor from sneering at the foolishness of his own soldiers, whose faces were free of the fear of the pestilence for the moment. They leaned against their horses or one another and laughed, slapping their thighs or their fellows' backs as if our journey through this stricken land were nothing but a dream.

"Are you sure this is a good idea, my lord?" Sir Andrew asked, looking stern as he eyed the Spanish soldiers.

The Black Prince gave him a sideways glance. "You worry too much, Andrew. I don't know how my father suffers your presence without wanting to cut his own throat." The prince lifted his chin arrogantly. "Everyone in this region is dead or dying of the pestilence. Who is left to attack us?"

Sir Andrew shrugged and turned away.

I tugged at George's arm to make him sit down beside me. The raucous energy of our camp made me nervous and the feverish heat of the fire seemed all too infectious. Only Sir Andrew and Henry seemed unaffected by the spectacle before them as they stood with their arms crossed at the edge of the fire's circle. The Spanish soldiers, dark like Gracias, were clapping and smiling but I noticed they kept their gaze trained on the prince at all times.

It was only after the soldiers grew too tired or too drunk to stand that Gracias finally ended his act and signaled to his soldiers that it was time to rest. George had fallen asleep a few songs past and his head rested against my arm. I shifted my weight against the log and guided him to my lap. I vowed to stay awake even as I closed my eyes and smelled the salt of the sea as it mixed with the sweet aroma of the fire.

"We must go!" someone hissed in my ear as a hand pressed against my mouth. I was startled but unable to cry out. I felt the terror in my throat as I struggled to clear away the cobwebs of sleep from my thoughts. *What does the prince want?*

It was dark, as the fire had burned itself out. I could not see anything at first and panicked for a moment that the prince had taken George, but I felt his weight against my stomach and heard his sleepy moan as I struggled.

"Stop it!" the voice commanded. "You'll wake them up!" The accent was foreign, I realized, not certain that I should be relieved. I had been listening to this voice for most of the night. I grabbed at the hand that covered my mouth and finally was able to make out the minstrel's dark eyes, suddenly stern beneath his bushy eyebrows. I thought of the mayor's note as my hand trembled against his. *Can I trust this man? What choice do I have?*

I pulled his hand away and pointed to George's sleeping form. "He comes with me."

Gracias smiled in amusement. "Well, you certainly give orders like a princesa." And just as quickly his smile vanished. "Wake him and do not make any noise. I do not know where the prince is."

I shook George gently and held my own hand against his mouth as I whispered for him to be still. As my eyes were adjusting to the darkness, I could see the soldiers sprawled out in the clearing, some snoring loudly. Many of them had used their shields for beds. A few of the horses had loosened their tied reins and had drifted to the edge of the woods. They were content as they munched on the long grass. The minstrel was right—I did not see the prince. I wondered if he had wandered down to the beach to create his own burning pyres as I had seen him that night from my window in the castle.

I heard what could have been the hoot of an owl, but it was just Gracias by our horses, motioning for George and me to mount. The two Spanish soldiers tiptoed through the sleeping men, ensuring that all were asleep. I grabbed the sack of clothes that I tied to my horse's saddle. It contained a few of the princess's dresses and two clean tunics for George. I led George gently past the few glowing embers that remained of the fire. He rubbed his eyes as if still dazed.

Suddenly Sir Andrew appeared from the woods and stood behind Gracias.

"*¿Son usted con nosotros?* Are you coming, sir?" Gracias asked pleasantly, as if inviting Sir Andrew on a hunt.

"No." Sir Andrew smiled. He looked positively happy. "But take Henry, he will help protect the princess." Henry, dressed in his worn leather armor, stepped from the shadows but did not look at me. I felt myself blush and was thankful that it was dark.

"Tell the mayor thank you for me," Sir Andrew said quietly as he shook the minstrel's hand. "I need to wait for the prince."

We galloped blindly in the darkness, thrashing our horses to spur them onto the rocky path that they had trod only hours ago. George clung to my waist. Henry was in front of me and in front of him the minstrel led. The two Spanish soldiers rode behind, yelling to each other, but I did not understand their foreign tongue.

After an hour of hard riding we stopped to allow our horses a short rest. Their mouths were flecked with froth and their bodies lathered in a damp sweat.

"That seemed too *fácil*, princesa," Gracias said as we sat on our horses in the middle of the road. In the dim moonlight, I saw a fine sheen of sweat shining on Gracias's face. "I do not trust your Black Prince," he continued. "He has the eyes of an animal."

Nor do I, I thought as my horse pawed skittishly at the ground. That is when we heard the squeaks—a hysterical chorus filled the air. The horses began to turn and buck as black rats—hundreds of them—swarmed around their legs.

"I'll show them my amulet!" George shouted above our yells. He must have had it out for only a minute when Henry screamed at George to put it away. "You are making the rats wild!" Henry yelled.

Henry was right. The rats were now leaping to reach George's hand, as if he held a fine morsel of food.

"Hold your reins!" Gracias commanded as he leaned from his saddle to swat at the rats with his shield. His bells tinkled shrilly in the frenzy. The two Spanish soldiers did the same, directing their horses in circles to mow down the rats at their thicker clusters. Thousands of beady eyes flashed in the moonlight and sharp teeth gleamed in the carpet of darkness around the horses' hooves.

I lifted my legs up and grabbed at George to do the same. Our horse bucked and I screamed as I felt myself slipping from the saddle. I threw my arms around its neck and yelled for George to hold me around the waist as our horse reared again. A rat was clinging to one of the horse's front legs with its teeth.

"We need to get on higher ground!" Henry yelled as he swung his sword erratically. "They are piling on top of one another!"

Henry was right, and the amulet seemed to be the object of their fury.

"Give me your amulet, George!" I screamed, as I grabbed at him again, searching for the chain to yank from his neck.

"Stop it, Nell! We need it! The rats don't like it because of its power to protect us," George insisted, pushing my hands away.

"¡Sígame! Follow me!" Gracias shouted, batting away at the fresh onslaught. His horse whinnied and pawed at the air before lurching blindly forward. Our horses did the same. I tried not to notice the agonizing squeals of the rats trampled beneath our horses' hooves.

We rode through the darkness even faster than before, this time taking no care of the tree branches that whipped across our faces or arms. Gracias's bells pounded out our pace. I felt George's face pressed into my back as his arms encircled my waist like a tight sash.

Soon we were riding uphill and our horses slowed

against the strain of the incline. Gracias had taken us to the top of a bluff, a few hundred feet higher than the woods surrounding us. From its top I could see the moonlight shimmer off the ocean's surface as it spread far off in the distance. All around us was the utter blackness of the woods. We listened to the night, but all I heard was our labored breathing.

"I believe we lost them, Nell," Gracias said quietly, turning to appraise me. His eyes looked black in the shadows.

"I am the...princess," I began without earnestness. I did not know if I was supposed to play the part still.

Henry was next to me, his horse brushing against mine. His hand clutched the hilt of his sword.

"It's all right, soldier," Gracias said. His bells tinged softly as he shifted his weight in his saddle. "I know the princess is dead. I was asked to save you from your fate."

"But how?" I asked. "You were coming from the south, from Castile..."

Gracias smiled mischievously. "The mayor's birds are faster than any man or beast. He sent me a message, as he knew Prince Pedro was anxious for me to greet you. Your Black Prince does not have many amigos here."

Fear stirred in my gut again. "What will the mayor

have you do with us?" I asked, glad that at least Henry had
a sword.

Gracias shook his head. "The mayor is a good man. If
it were up to me, I would ensure that the prince could
not use you for his purposes again." Gracias' eyes were
suddenly hard and his voice thick with meaning. George
gave a little cry.

"But it is not up to you, sir," Henry replied boldly. He
was slowly drawing his sword. The two Spanish soldiers
suddenly flanked Henry.

"*Guarde en su sitio su espada.* Put your sword away,
soldier," Gracias commanded. "You are right. It is not
up to me. The mayor asked that I direct you back to
Bordeaux. He will tell you what your futures hold."

I touched Henry on the arm, encouraging him to set
aside the sword. For the moment, it seemed, we were safe.

the monk

WE SPENT THE NIGHT on the hillside, straining to hear the squeals of the rats, but all we heard was the soft whispering of leaves in the pre-dawn October breeze. George had fallen asleep and I cradled him with my arm to keep him from slipping from the saddle. I could feel Gracias peering over at me, and when I met his stare he tried to reassure me, but he wore an empty smile. His soldiers moved around the edge of our bluff, peering down into its wooded slopes to detect any movement in the darkness. Henry stayed by my side but said nothing. He reminded me of an animal, ready to spring at the slightest provocation.

Fear extinguished all temptation to drowse in my saddle and soon I began to dread even the silence. Waiting for the return of the rats wound my nerves. At least, when we were under attack, there was no time for thought.

"The rats belong to the prince," I announced. The secret was too horrible to keep. I needed to share this horror.

"Are you saying that your prince is a sorcerer?" Gracias asked, looking at me sharply. His eyes were black stones in the moonlight. He cocked his head and pulled at his black beard as if intrigued by the notion.

A sorcerer? I had never thought about the prince in that light. A new fear stabbed at my gut. Perhaps that would explain his nocturnal outings and his sacks filled with live creatures, but I ignored his question, as it was too terrible to imagine.

"I saw them," I continued. "He kept them in the dungeon at the castle in Bordeaux. I dreamed about them, too." I did not look at Gracias, but instead stared into the darkness. "He would send them out to hunt people." I thought of George's friends—the little French girls—and prayed that they were safe.

"Only a princess can dream about the future. Are you saying that you have the power of a princess?" Gracias asked mockingly. "Your prince must be a true follower of the dark arts to command such *criaturas*. How could this be? He is the son of your king."

"I'm only telling you what I know!" I answered defiantly.

"Let her be," Henry interrupted. "She served the princess honorably. Nell never took any liberties," he added firmly.

I looked at him gratefully, although I knew the darkness masked my expression.

"Besides, how else would you explain the attack of the rats?" Henry asked. "Rats are afraid of their own shadows."

"Not if they are hungry or believe that they are being threatened," Gracias shot back. His bells chimed his skepticism. "Anyway, the prince will follow us, of course, as soon as the soldiers are sober enough to ride. We best be ready and stop all *conversación*," he ordered, all teasing gone from his voice.

I shivered sympathetically for the soldiers. They had come to France to protect the princess on her journey to Castile. They had never bargained to be the weapons of the prince's demented scheme. I began to worry that the prince was truly mad.

We left at dawn and guided our horses down the hillside path that had been long abandoned. Our horses tread carefully through the growth, stepping over a loose vine or the thorny shrubs that clutched at their ankles, already sore and raw from the bites of the rats. The jostling movement was painful, for we had been on our horses for many hours without relief. Gracias had insisted that we take the path through the woods instead of the one along the coast, as that route was open and unprotected. I trembled in the cold chill of the October air that had dampened our clothes and brows. The sunlight that pierced the still thick canopy of the trees was weak and the tang of the dew on the leaf-covered ground was sharp against my nose.

George's voice was still weary with sleep. His head brushed against my back with each step we took. "Where are we going?" he asked.

"I don't know, George. We need to ask Gracias," I replied. My heart began to beat wildly as I anticipated an answer.

For the moment, Gracias said nothing. His soldiers, who followed behind me began to shout questions at Gracias, too, although I did not understand what they were saying.

"Do you have a plan?" Henry asked over their noise. He sounded impatient as his horse nudged the flank of Gracias's horse.

I suddenly realized that Henry had cast himself as a traitor when he joined us. *Why did he do this?* The prince would be looking for us and would not be kind to anyone who advanced our escape.

"*Por supuesto* I have a plan!" Gracias shot back, giving a stern look at his men. "Do you think the mayor and I would kidnap a *princesa* without a strategy? The mayor has identified a number of agents to work on our behalf to get you all back to Bordeaux. The first is a monk. I am taking you to him now." Gracias turned in his saddle to throw me a meaningful look. "Perhaps this is a good thing. The monk can use the power of good against the sorcerer powers of the prince."

"A sorcerer!" George exclaimed, suddenly awake. "It's a good thing I have my amulet." I looked over my shoulder to see George grasping at it beneath his tunic.

I didn't trust the amulet, and I wondered how I could separate George from it, as the prince had one that made a matching pair. There could be no good in that. I concentrated on finding a way to convince George that the amulet was bad. And I did not want a second visit by the rats.

"Come along." Gracias waved. "The monk is at least an hour's ride from here. Let us hope he can provide us with breakfast."

We arrived at an hour when the farmers should have been in the fields, picking grapes or guiding the sheep and goats to pasture, but the village was quiet and seemed starkly alone.

"Something is wrong here," Gracias warned, signaling our horses to slow to a stop at the end of the dirt path that spilled into the village square. I glanced nervously around for rats but none were visible. Was this village deserted like so many we passed on our way to Castile?

A small stone church commanded the center of the cobbled square. Its spire had toppled and a bird's nest was nestled in its place. I cringed at the mournful sound of an abandoned door, squeaking, as if bitter, at the teasing push of the breeze. We stared silently at the huddle of wood-and-thatch houses that lined the square, on both sides of the church, like embracing arms. Many of the houses had small barns at their backs or dirt yards full of chickens. I shivered, despite the warmth I felt on my shoulders and back from the sun that had finally called forth its heat. Only the birds of the woods dared break the silence with their loud chattering. Perhaps only the birds were left to share this part of the world with us.

We all jumped in our saddles when a young monk slammed open the doors of the church with a force that could splinter wood. He stood in the church's threshold and brushed his hands against his brown robe as if they were wet. His head was shaved in a tonsure. His cheeks looked sunken and his eyes shone unnaturally above dark hollows. He appeared hungry and tired, yet emitted a singular intensity.

"*Bonjour*, Sir Gracias," he said, blinking up at us as if he just remembered why we were here. "*Pardonner* us that we cannot give you an appropriate greeting. I am Friar Phillipe. We expected your arrival."

Gracias' soldiers were looking around suspiciously and spurred their horses to trot around the square. They slowed to peer into windows and doorways and down still, shadowed alleyways between the silent houses. The village seemed to be holding its breath.

Henry was beside me again. His eyes were clouded, as if he sensed what was wrong. We both did.

Gracias was leaning to the side to stare at the monk and then suddenly bowed. His bells mimicked the trills of the birds.

"Thank you, Friar, but where are the villagers?"

The monk's tranquil expression did not change, although he closed his eyes, as if summoning the strength to answer.

He released a loud sigh. "The town is a victim of the pestilence. The villagers are either sick or nursing their stricken families. I myself have been here but two weeks, sent to replace the parish priest, who was one of the first to fall ill." He lifted his arm, his robe hanging from it like a wing, as the monk directed our gaze to sweep the village square.

"You will see no marks or watchmen at these homes. My order requires the charitable care of the poor, under all circumstances," he explained.

The plague. My heart was pounding and my temples were throbbing. *Will we ever be safe?* We spent the night on our horses to escape the prince's rats, only to be delivered to another dying village.

"George," I whispered. I needed to know that he was listening.

"It's okay, Nell," he whispered back. "I have the amulet."

That hardly gave me comfort.

"*Bien*," Gracias said cheerfully. "We have done our part, Friar, which is to deliver the princess to you. My soldiers and I will be on our way back to Castile."

"You are going to leave us here?" I asked, incredulous despite myself. In my mind, I suddenly saw an image of the prince, dressed in his full black armor, galloping toward us, the black plume of his wake made up of an army of rats. Once Gracias left, we would have only Henry to help us get back to Bordeaux. And that was if we did not catch the pestilence first. I struggled against the hysteria I felt rising in my throat.

"My duty has been completed, princess. No need to give me thanks."

"We'll be better off without him," Henry declared before I could protest. "I don't trust him."

"Nor I you, sir," Gracias shot back. "But that is all water under the drawbridge now. It's best that you maintain that attitude if you wish to escort the princesa back safely." Gracias was smiling again, that infuriating smile that implied that he knew everything.

"*C'est bien*" the monk interjected. "You will only be here for a day, as your next guide will be along tomorrow morning to collect you. Today I could use the soldier and the boy in the fields, as much of our grape harvesting has been neglected. The princess shall rest in the church and perhaps say some prayers for the recovery of this village. It appears that my own prayers are not enough to atone for its sins."

I nodded, almost paralyzed by a sense of doom. *What*

choice do we have? I could not command Gracias to stay nor make him take us with him. There was nothing to be done except to send George to the fields and pray that we lasted the night.

"You, sir, are heartless," I accused, clutching the reins of my horse in my fury. "So it may seem, princesa," Gracias replied, his tone grave. He turned away from me to address the monk.

"If you don't mind, Friar, we will refresh our horses and take some nourishment for our journey."

The monk nodded. "Of course. My kitchen is full."

"Well, this is *adios* then," Gracias said, swiveling his horse back in my direction. He called like an owl to get the attention of his soldiers. They quickly reappeared at his side. Now his eyes and smile seemed more amused than hostile.

"We will pray for your safe arrival, princesa, and for the preservation of your king's crown. Beware the world in which your sorcerer prince should command."

We were in the vineyards by midmorning. We each had a bucket in our hands and I wore an apron over the princess's soiled dress. Its once-brilliant yellow lions were now brown and scraggly like cats caught in a rainstorm. It was Henry who saw the apron on a peg in the church's kitchen as we were eating the brown bread and porridge that the monk placed before us on the table. He smiled as we hesitated, as the large portions embarrassed us.

"*S'il vous plaît*, the food will soon spoil. Someone must eat it," he said softly. He closed his eyes as he paused to listen to the morning call of the roosters. He covered his face with his hand and sighed, as if gathering strength.

"You'll find buckets in the churchyard," he said to Henry and George. "The vineyards, although small, are hardy," he added, a touch of pride in his voice. "Pass through the grove of trees behind the church and you will find them. Princess, you may make yourself comfortable in our church, which you should find cool and quiet. I regret that I cannot offer you better shelter."

"Do not worry, Friar," I reassured him quickly. "We are extremely grateful."

Although I did not tell him that I did not plan on staying in the church. I knew I would have gone mad sitting in this kitchen alone all day, wondering what was happening to George and Henry. My vow was all I had now—nothing would ever separate George and me.

The monk was right. The vines were ripe yet still clung strongly to tree branches that had been used to create a trellislike wall for the grapes to grow along. There were three long rows of them that stretched down to the valley. I could see a stream, perhaps a quarter mile away, sparkling like a diamond in the sunlight. The green valley rose again from the stream's opposite bank. The world looked so peaceful here.

We each chose a separate row. I was in the middle, yet we picked side by side, glancing at one another through the plump or slightly shriveled grapes that seemed to ache to be plucked from their vines. The work felt good, for it required no thought, and for a few moments I could pretend that we were safe. I did not want to think about what the monk would do with these grapes, as were leaving in the morning. *Will he and the few healthy villagers that remained do the work to preserve them or make wine?*

"Look at my fingers, Nell!" George called from the other side of the row of vines. He held up his splayed hand. The tips of his fingers were purple.

"Lick it off, George!" I said, a bit alarmed, as it looked as if his fingers might stay that color forever.

"Don't be silly, Nell. If I lick them now, they'll just get purple again. It will wear away." He cocked his head as he stared at me through the vine-entwined lattice of sticks. His amused smile exposed his missing front teeth. "Look at your own fingers," he suggested.

I turned my hand over and was surprised to see the evidence of my own grape picking. For a moment, I felt a stitch of guilt because I did not change into one of the other dresses that I had stuffed into my sack. I knew it was silly of me but worried that I had broken my vow to honor the princess's memory by harvesting in her dress. Never mind that the dress was worn and bedraggled from our escape from the prince. But the other dresses were still clean, I reasoned. No reason to soil more than one. What would the monk think if he caught me? He did not seem to have the strength for one more prayer for one more sinner.

"Well, at least one could tell that we are related by our fingers," I relented. I was warmed by the sun and the beauty of the vineyards and the momentary joy of sharing this simple task of picking grapes. And besides, it was so good to see George smile.

"Henry, let's have a look at your hands!" I called over to the row on the other side of me. Henry was farther ahead than George and me, and I realized that he had been silent since we entered the arbor.

He looked back at us and waved a purple hand over his head, but he did not smile. I watched as he pushed a strand of his brown hair away from his eyes with the back of his wrist. He was wearing only his tunic and stockings, as he had left his armor back in the church kitchen. He suddenly looked like a young man to me, barely older than I.

"Are you all right, Henry?" I asked, as if anyone could be all right under our circumstances. But right now, the sun was in the sky, the birds of the woods were chattering happily, and the branches of the arbor suggested a fortress around us—one made of sticks, but still a fortress. And the air was dizzyingly sweet with the odor of fermenting grapes.

"I'm going to move down the row, Nell," George said. "My bucket is nearly full. I will be back after I empty it."

I nodded but kept my eyes on Henry as I approached him. He turned his back to me as he continued to pick.

"Henry? What is it?" I asked. A nervousness made my voice tremble just a little. I reached to touch him on the arm but paused when he replied.

"I have done you wrong, Nell," he said. Now he turned and looked me fully in the face. His brown eyes glistened in the sunlight. A welt, probably earned from a tree branch during last night's ride, crossed his left cheek. He looked so vulnerable.

"What do you mean? You have placed your own life in danger by helping us escape the prince. For that I am extremely thankful," I gushed. For I could not imagine what I would be doing now if it were just George and me. Although Henry was only one soldier, I was grateful to have someone to share my burden.

He shook his head. "No. I mean many those two years ago, back in England. That scared, stupid boy who dragged the death cart for your parents—that was me."

I couldn't breathe. Suddenly I was there again, in that mud-filled alley in London, when a thin boy with wide dark eyes asked for my help in collecting my dead parents. I could see that boy in Henry's face, just as I thought I had seen it back on the ship. He was looking down at his feet now, just as he had that day that changed our lives so drastically.

This time I did touch his arm. "That was not your fault," I insisted, my voice catching in my throat. "You were doing the king's bidding, as all the pestilence watch-men were required to do."

"No. It was horrible, taking the loved ones from their families while they grieved. If it were now, I would pass by your house, despite its markings." He looked up at me fiercely, his chin raised and his face taut.

"I know, Henry." I smiled, my chest suddenly feeling light at the thought of having someone else in the world. "Let's empty our buckets and get a cup of water from the well in the churchyard. George must be there already."

But George wasn't there. We ran into the churchyard, scattering the chickens as they clucked indignantly.

"George!" I called into the kitchen, not wanting to raise my voice for fear of alerting the monk of my whereabouts.

The air was leaden with silence.

"Let's look in the square. We can see most of the village from there," Henry reasoned, tugging my hand to guide me back into the yard. The chickens had already regrouped and were pecking at the pieces of bread that the monk must have scattered earlier. We went down the alley between the church and a neighboring house whose shutters were closed tight. In a moment, we stood in the square beneath the warm October sun. It was empty and quiet, as if the cursed village had swallowed up George.

I looked around, willing George to appear. I could feel the sweat of fear on my forehead and the stickiness of my fingers against my palms.

"Don't worry, Nell. He must be with the monk," Henry assured me.

It was then that we heard a young boy's cry, a cry full of pain and anguish.

"George!" I screamed, turning in the direction of the heartbreaking wail—a small thatched house three away from the church. Its door was open.

I grabbed Henry's hand. Despite the short distance, I could barely breathe when we reached its threshold. The sunlight that cut between our shoulders splashed across three figures—the monk, kneeling in prayer, a young boy with terrified eyes lying on a straw mat, and George, with his hand cradling the boy's head as his other hand held a cup to the boy's lips.

I suddenly felt cold to my bones. "George," I gasped. "Get away from the boy."

I cringed at the harshness of my words, but the boy had the plague.

"B-but Nell," George stammered, as if shocked. "The boy would not drink anything till I helped him."

"Friar," Henry interrupted. "Does this boy not have the pestilence? George is clean!" Henry said accusingly.

The monk slowly lifted his bald head, his hands still clasped in prayer. "Your brother is a healer, princess. He has much to do in this village today." The monk's gaze fell upon George and the sick boy. "Your brother has a gift," he continued. "He has already convinced three children to drink. And when he left them, their fevers had cooled and they soon fell into a restful sleep. Would you not have wanted the same for your parents, child?"

So George had told the priest. I threw George a murderous look.

Henry took my elbow. "Let him be, Nell. I had watched many die as we waited in the streets with the cart. None looked as peaceful as this boy."

Henry was right. The boy's initial look of terror, possibly from our bursting into the room, was gone. A sleepy, serene expression now occupied his small face. There was nothing for me to do but turn away.

That night, in the barn by the vineyards, I held myself tight as we lay in our beds of straw. I thought about how Henry and I had returned to finish our work plucking grapes as George made the sick rounds with Friar Phillipe. When he was finally returned to me, I anxiously searched his face and body for signs of the fever, or the black roses—the horrifying bruises that bloomed and bulged near the armpits or groin—that marked the pestilence.

"You don't feel hot?" I interrogated George nonetheless.

He shook his head and rewarded me with his tooth-less grin. "No, Nell. Please. I am okay. Just a little tired." He pulled out his amulet and rubbed it between his hands. "I think this is helping the village," he said in won-der. "As long as I have it, maybe I can make people well."

Henry eyed the amulet suspiciously and, with a snort, rolled away from us to sleep.

I pulled George close to me. "We will ask the monk about your amulet tomorrow. Let us find out what he believes about its power."

George nodded and closed his eyes and, within min-utes, was fast asleep. Sleep didn't tarry for me either, as I too felt physically exhausted. I woke only once, when I thought I heard the soft scratching of rats on the other side of the barn's walls. I held my breath and waited, but heard nothing. Yet the sound of tiny paws burrowing into the dirt filled my dreams.

the gravedigger

DAWN HAD BARELY SHAKEN the world awake when Friar Phillipe rapped on the barn door.

"Princess," he called. "I have packed a basket of food for you and your companions. The gravedigger will be here anytime now."

Henry was putting on his armor while George was sleepily pulling pieces of straw from his hair as he sat on the pallet. I had already decided that the dress I had been wearing would make do until we reached Bordeaux. I hurried to open the door. The monk's gaze dropped to the ground when I looked into his shadowed face.

"Thank you, Friar. We are so very grateful." I winced at the suffering that seemed to pull his features downward. How awful for him to be left behind.

"*Je suis désolé*…I'm sorry I could not offer you better lodging, princess, but I dared not take a chance with any of the homes. I don't know yet which ones are safe." He looked up, but past me, into the barn, as his fingers worked the rope of his robe like a rosary.

"We were very comfortable," I replied. "You have much greater burdens to worry about."

He nodded and then, surprisingly, stepped around me as if to enter the barn.

"The boy," he said quickly. "May I have a strand of his hair, to assist me with the healing?" His eyes pleaded with me for a moment before they locked on to George.

"His hair?" I repeated. I, too, turned to look at George, standing now beneath the barn's loft, which was piled with more hay. Straw was still sticking to his black stockings as he waved a hello to the monk. The sunlight streaming in through the open shutters lit George from behind like an apparition. Henry simply frowned as he stared at the monk.

"You will be leaving in a few minutes, but if you leave me a token of the boy, his healing powers may continue to sustain us," he reasoned. His hand slipped into the pocket of his robe.

I looked from George to Henry. *The monk is our friend,*

I reasoned. He would not do anything to hurt George. And I myself had witnessed this strange power in George that never presented itself until yesterday. The monk was now fidgeting with the object in his pocket.

George approached the monk, who had yet to cross the barn's threshold. He pulled his amulet from his tunic as he walked. "Should I leave this with you, Friar? It was made by a blacksmith in England to protect us." George held it close to the monk's face.

The monk's eyes widened and he stepped back. "*Aucun merci*. No thank you, child." He pushed the amulet away with his hand. "Such charms are too easily changed. Your hair is all I need." The monk slowly reached toward George's head.

"Let me assist you, Friar," Henry interrupted. I could see the tension in his movements, although his voice was free of any sign of impatience. He strode over and held out his hand. "Your knife, Friar? I will cut you a lock."

The monk looked at Henry in surprise and slowly removed a small carving knife from his pocket.

"Come here, George," Henry instructed. "I'll give the monk a small strand to protect you from a tonsure." Henry smiled then, and playfully boxed George on the ear. George grinned nervously but did what he was told. The monk's face was pale as he watched this odd ceremony. Tiny dust motes floated in the air of the barn, making the entire scene seem unreal.

"I'm stepping outside to get some fresh air," I said. I felt shaken and I was unsure why, and I did not want to watch Henry cut off a clump of George's hair. I walked and paused in the open grass between the barn and the churchyard, as I willed the sunlight and the smell of morning to warm my clammy hands. Our horses were munching on a shared bale of hay in the churchyard. The monk must have given it to them before he came to the barn. It was then that I turned to walk to the back of the barn, needing to reassure myself of one more nagging fear.

My heart stopped as I reached the barn wall. We had slept by its interior side. The edge of grass had been stripped here to reveal a trough, six inches deep into the earth, six feet long along the edge of the barn, as if dug by tiny paws. I cried out as I dropped to my knees to see if a section of the barn wall had been breached. The wall appeared unbroken, even though the wood had been gnawed to splinters where it met the dirt.

"Is that him?" George asked in wonder, squinting into the horizon of the dirt road that led to the village square.

I could just barely make out a figure, as its form was still protected by the shadows cast by the canopy of the trees that grew up to the road, trees always ready to reclaim even this small strip of civilization. Whoever, or whatever, it was moved with a slow, consistent diligence.

"It must be the gravedigger," Henry said with certainty. "He moves like a man who need not fear other men. Only the gravediggers are feared as much as death." I looked at Henry's long face, but he was staring gloomily ahead.

The monk had left us in the square as he went to begin his sick rounds. A fresh lock of George's hair was in his pocket. We had our basket of food, and our horses were fresh and nervous again, sensing that we were ready to begin our journey. I did not tell Henry and George about what I had found at the back of the barn. I am not sure why, except that somehow I feared that it would only bring us more bad luck. Instead I stood silently in the square, standing on top of the smooth cobblestones, the church at our backs. The ring of silent houses surrounded us, each holding its breath, as if waiting for us to leave.

"George, did you meet any villagers yesterday that were not sick?" I asked, almost in a whisper in case they were listening.

George cocked his head. A tuft of his blond hair stood up where Henry had taken the knife. "I did not, Nell, but I think Friar Phillipe took me only to the houses where everyone was sick."

I nodded. I did not know what to believe.

"I can hear his approach," Henry announced to quiet us. We said nothing, but listened to the rhythmic squeak of the cart's wooden wheels. "It's a high squeak," Henry said after a few minutes. "The cart must be empty."

George picked up the food basket, and Henry and I each led our horses around the square to stand at the village's entrance. We must have looked like quite a sorry welcome to the gray-bearded man, dressed in a dirty brown tunic with torn red stockings. He pulled a large wooden cart by two handles. His arms were thickly muscled and his eyes a lively blue. I wondered if we all gaped when he finally stood before us and dropped the handles of the cart to bow.

"Princess, it is my honor to escort you to the *cimetière*." He smiled the unperturbed smile of a child. Only George could have matched it.

We stared rudely, until Henry echoed, "To the grave-yard, sir? We are supposed to be going to Bordeaux."

"Yes." The gravedigger winked. "But I am to take you

only as far as the cimetière. No one promised you *une ligne droite*, a straight line to Bordeaux, did they? That would not have been wise. Even a gravedigger knows that."

Henry scowled. "What did that Gracias scoundrel get us into? Nothing has made sense since we left the prince," I heard him mutter under his breath. He threw a suspicious glance back into the village.

"Perhaps that is why we are still safe," I offered, throwing him a warning look instead of reaching for his hand to calm him as I wanted to do. But I knew that, as I was acting as the princess, such gestures were forbidden. "The Black Prince may be on the road we took from Bordeaux as we speak," I added. I wished I believed it.

Henry only looked at me, unconvinced.

"Your cart is empty," George pointed out, seemingly mesmerized by the gravedigger.

"I finished a collection last night," the gravedigger replied matter-of-factly. He then lifted his head and sniffed at the air. "Ah, I'll be back tonight, but the number is less than I thought." His brazen blue eyes twinkled at George. He then swung around to me.

"I see that I cleaned out my cart for naught." He lifted his chin at our horses. "Unless the boy wishes to get in. We have fifteen miles or so to travel."

"That's quite all right, sir," I answered abruptly. "The boy will ride with me."

We rode for hours, along well-worn trails cooled by the thick awning of forest trees. Trees massive in girth and muscle hemmed us in on both sides and I imagined I could feel the weight of their presence on my shoulders. The smell of damp earth filled our nostrils as we breathed air usually reserved for the creatures of the natural world. We listened for the sounds of horses and stopped periodically to touch the earth, but we felt or heard nothing but the sounds of wild animals. The few villages we passed, although occupied, quickly became deserted when the cart approached. One look at the gravedigger and the adults would toss their children under their arms and bolt their doors. I began to think our gravedigger was better protection than the Black Prince's fifty men.

The gravedigger pulled the cart at a quick pace, never grimacing at the load. For being a man who usually keeps company with the dead, he was surprisingly talkative. George, of course, was charmed. Henry ignored the chatter and was intent on peering into the forest. A nervous sweat shone on his forehead. I guessed he thought that the gravedigger would not be much of an ally under an attack.

"How old are you?" George asked, probably confused by the gravedigger's gray beard yet jet-black hair. The gravedigger's face was deeply lined, though.

"As old as the four *pestes*, the pestilences," he replied, "which makes me the oldest man in the *monde*."

"Aren't you afraid of death?" George asked. "Nell and I hated the cart when it came to our house in England." I gasped. George seemed to find comfort in telling the whole world about our parents. Henry frowned and looked away.

"George," I interrupted a bit harshly. "There is no reason to tell everyone about the death of your parents. People will fear you." I tried to convey my real meaning in my voice. He must remember that until we were safe in England, I was the princess and Nell was nothing but a sorely missed sister.

George nodded in an exaggerated way, his blond hair flipping up and down with the movements, but the gravedigger did not seem to hear us.

"I must be immune to death by now, *garçon*. I'm all weeped out." The gravedigger suddenly stopped. "*J'ai senti*, I smelled the pestilence on you just now, on that teasing breeze. Not the poison vapors, but the ombre the Black Death casts on souls." He looked around us quickly and ran from horse to horse, sniffing the air again. The horses whined and backed away.

"What is it that you are wearing, boy?" he demanded. "Suddenly you reek of death. I know it's not your spirit."

My hand instinctively covered my chest. The amulet. "Show it to him, George," I ordered. George meekly leaned around me, pulling the amulet from his tunic.

The gravedigger nodded. "Best be rid of that," he said, and we continued on our path.

"What happened here?" George asked in wonderment. We stood on the rim of a wide valley, its gentle slopes marred by the burned out trunks of forest trees. The air still reeked of the stinging odor of a ferocious blaze that had blackened the earth, searing away the grass and shrubs that had once carpeted the forest floor. In the center of this valley cut a small stream. Its waters ran black, as if a recent rainfall had carried away the charred pieces of bark and dirt that now lined its dead banks. Within these blackened borders lay the graveyard—patches of raw earth rent with gaping holes like the pustules of England's plague.

"This is the cimetière, garçon. This is where we stop and wait for the carts," the gravedigger replied, pushing a tangle of his matted black hair away from his sticky forehead.

"Who did this?" I asked. I realized I was trembling in my saddle.

"The lords of two châteaus that surround this forest had their soldiers round up the farmers and any other bodies that were still healthy enough to walk. Too many people were dying, and there was no room, left in the small cimetières to bury them. They burned this site to make more room, and to move the dead away from the living." He turned to look at me, his startling blue eyes a vivid contrast to the devastation in front of us.

"What are we supposed to do now, sir?" Henry asked. He shifted in his saddle, as his horse was skittish. No living thing feels comfortable in the midst of death it seemed. Henry patted his horse on the neck and whispered something soothing in its ear.

"We wait for the bodies," he answered, as if it was the most normal thing in the world. "But now, I understand *vous avez des provisions*, you have provisions?" he asked, his voice tinged with the immediacy of a child's.

"Yes. Let's have something to eat," I agreed. I would have done anything to take our eyes away from those burial pits. "Can we choose a spot that does not offer this view?" I asked.

"I will find one, princess," Henry answered quickly.

He turned his horse to face into the woods. I smiled at Henry's back. He was a young soldier of stormy humors. I wondered, *What demons is he wrestling with, besides the knowledge that the Black Prince is hunting us?*

"As long as I can still see early arrivals," the gravedigger agreed, reminding me of what was immediately important.

Henry had found a small clearing, only yards away from the forest path. We walked the horses through the brush and tied them to a tree at the clearing's edge. The sun warmed the tops of our heads as we removed the morsels that the monk had packed for us—brown bread, chunks of cheese, and two flasks of mead. He had even provided a bunch of the green grapes that we had picked just yesterday. We settled down and, for a moment, the thick foliage sheltering us and the chattering of the forest birds protected our mood from the graveyard beyond.

We ate in silence, and only when the gravedigger had taken his final swallow did he narrow his eyes at George. "Let me see that charm you are wearing, garçon."

George was hesitant, but slowly pulled the amulet from his tunic.

"Take it off. I mean to examine it," he urged impatiently.

"It's mine," George reminded him as he dropped the amulet into the gravedigger's outstretched palm. The gravedigger rubbed it between his hands, as if warming it. He then brought it close to his weathered face, only inches from his eyes.

"I've seen many like this to ward off the pestilence. Most are harmless and serve no purpose beyond giving its bearer a false *confiance*. But this one..." He shuddered. "This bears an evil imprint. I would bury this now in the woods."

"No!" George cried, leaping up to grab the thing. "It is mine. It has protected us! Please, Nell. Make him give it back!"

I grabbed George by the arm and tried to gently pull him down beside me. "Forgive the boy," I asked. "He has been excitable since he lost his own parents and sister to the pestilence." I tried to give George a stern look. He turned his head away from me peevishly. "I must remind him of her."

"Give it here, sir," Henry offered. "And I'll ensure it's done." He stood and extended his hand, as if he were accepting a small gift, but his voice was firm.

"The blacksmith gave it to *me*," George muttered as he watched Henry push his way through the brush until all we saw were his movements caught by the sun that filtered through the gaps in the tree canopy.

"It doesn't endure the mark of a blacksmith, garçon. It casts something far more powerful," the gravedigger said, shaking his head.

"Please, George," I said angrily. "I trust the gravedigger. There is something about that amulet that makes me dream of rats."

We were interrupted by the blow of a horn. The gravedigger shot right up.

"What's this? An early arrival?" he asked. He scrambled from our tiny clearing through the forest rim to the pathway. George and I quickly followed.

Standing on the edge of the valley again, we spied a line of carts, one by one cresting the horizon on the other side. The carts made their own dark silhouettes against the gnarled hulks of the blackened tree line. Their pace was slow and often two people were sharing the load. I knew they must be filled.

"What are you to do now?" I asked, suddenly afraid to lose the man.

"I will greet them and help them with their obligations. They knew these people they carry. Their *coeurs*, their hearts, bear a much greater burden than mine."

"Should we help you?" George asked. His blue eyes were wide. He was obviously moved by the sight before us, enough to forget his anger with the gravedigger.

"No, garçon," the gravedigger answered before I could. "A band of merchants should be passing this way by sundown. You are to wait for them, as they will escort you and the princess into Bordeaux. It is only a day's ride from here."

We watched as the gravedigger picked up his own cart and maneuvered it down the hillside, past the burned-out remnants of trees and dried mud, into the valley below. Henry soon joined us as we watched the morbid procession.

"I don't want to watch," George said finally. "I am going to rest back in the clearing."

I didn't want him to watch this gruesome sight either. I kissed the top of his hair, which smelled of dirt and sunlight. "We will be here, waiting for the merchants. Call if you need me," I instructed.

Henry and I stood as if mesmerized as we stared at the scene below us. It was still a few hours from sundown.

"Henry, do you think this is the end of the world?" I asked as we watched cart after cart empty their contents into the pits. I couldn't call them people, the things in the carts, or I would have to cry out in despair. My parents had suffered the same horrific end. It was a blessing perhaps that from here they looked like bolts of dirty cloth. There was nothing to define these forms as man, woman, or child.

"No, Nell." Henry stood close to me. I could almost feel his shoulder touching mine. "This is another cleansing, although I can't imagine that it's one from God, as the priests like to tell us. I don't want to believe that God would have such loathing for us."

I wanted to question him further. I wanted to know what he thought the future would hold for us, as my spirit was dark, but George came crashing through the brush to reach us. He pointed toward the road as he ran, nearly tripping over his own feet.

"Nell! It's one of Gracias's soldiers, coming down the path!"

We whirled around. Sure enough, the larger, burly-shouldered soldier was coming at a brisk trot toward us. One hand gripped his reins and the other his sword.

We were frozen to the spot as his black horse came within yards of us before he stopped. Henry pulled out his sword. I pushed George behind me.

The soldier's face was drenched with sweat. It poured from beneath his helmet, plastering the stray ends of his black hair against his forehead and cheeks. His long, black beard looked oiled. He was gasping for breath.

"You must go," he croaked in a harsh English. "You cannot wait!"

Henry approached him cautiously. "Why, what is Gracias up to?" he asked suspiciously.

Yet the soldier said nothing as he grimaced, as if a sharp pain suddenly wracked his body. Before Henry took another step closer, the soldier tumbled from his saddle and fell to the ground. His body hit the dirt with a heavy thud. An arrow stood straight from his back, piercing him between his armored vest and shoulder.

"Oh no!" I cried, stepping back.

George scampered around me to touch the soldier's back. "I can't help him," he said sadly.

Henry was already running for the horses. "Come on, princess! Grab your pack. Come on, George!"

Henry crashed through the brush from the clearing, pulling our horses by their reins. Their eyes bulged with terror. Did they sense the rats, I wondered, pushing down my own rising panic? Henry lifted George onto my horse, and then heaved me onto the saddle. We were soon galloping along the rim of the valley, trusting that we would find the road to Bordeaux.

From the periphery of my eye, I could see the gravedigger in the valley below us, waving his arms frantically as empty carts stood behind him like sentinels next to the burying pits that checkered the valley's landscape.

I focused on the narrow road ahead that would take us back into the woods. I thought I heard the gravedigger's cry echo in the air behind us.

"*Attendez*! Wait! You cannot go without the merchants!"

the merchants

THE HOOVES OF OUR HORSES pounded many miles
of forest path. Neither of us dared to look back.
We held our reins tightly and kept our faces close
to our horses' thick necks; the smell of their sweat stung
our nostrils. George's thin, dirty arms were wrapped
around my waist. His head bumped into my back each
time our horse touched the ground.

The forest course was narrow on this side of the valley, and we had to flee in single file. It was darker here, as
the early evening sun did not have the power to penetrate
the forest's thick green awning, and the branches of the
lower trees reached across our path. Soon we were forced
to slow down, and Henry finally stopped, turning his
horse around with difficulty. Fresh welts marked his face.

"We don't know these woods, nor this trail, which doesn't appear well traveled," Henry panted. "I'm not sure that I trust us to find Bordeaux." I heard the lonely hoot of an owl in the distance, the only sound other than the chatterings of the winged creatures that were all around us. But no bird was visible through the matrix of trees that walled us in on both sides. At least it was cool, pausing in this place.

"Perhaps, in a little while, when we feel it is safe, we can trace our way back to the graveyard and wait for the merchants," I suggested. I agreed with Henry. This trail could just as well take us to the opposite coast of France. The princess had shown me a map before we left and I remembered my surprise at seeing that it touched two seas.

"I like that idea!" George piped in. "These woods are a little scary," he added as a shiver rode through his body. I looked down at his arms again, as he still clung to my waist. How did he get so dirty? Had he fallen?

"No, I think that would be too dangerous," Henry said, slipping out of his saddle. He began to pace from his horse to mine and back again. "Perhaps we can wait here for the merchants. Let them catch up to us. We are on their path, are we not?" He sounded as if he were speaking to himself.

"Or we simply can head west," I said. "Find our way to the coast and proceed north to Bordeaux. The gravedigger said we were only a day away."

Henry stopped pacing and looked at me as if I were daft. His eyebrows arched as he replied, "And stumble into the Black Prince's army?"

I sat straight up in my saddle, insulted. "Well then, we must wait right here. The gravedigger will point the merchants our way," I sniffed. Did he think he was the only one who had ideas, I wondered. George whimpered behind me.

"We will wait, then," Henry agreed. "But let's take our horses into the woods, away from the open trail."

We found a small clearing, a few hundred yards up the road, large enough to tie our horses so that they would be invisible to other travelers. I removed my sack from the saddle and placed it on the ground, making a pillow for George that was softer than the thick carpet of pine needles that would serve as our bedding. I lay next to George, while Henry crept closer to the road to keep watch for the merchants.

"Nell, do you think the merchants will find us?" he whispered nervously into my ear.

"I am sure they will," I said. "The gravedigger will

instruct them to catch up to us. Now close your eyes,"
I proposed, "and just listen to the forest. It has its own
lullaby." George nuzzled closer to me.

I could only see a few feet in front of me, now that
the shadows of the forest had merged with the early
evening darkness. I could not discern Henry, so I needed
to just trust that he was by the road, safe and watchful.

I closed my eyes and took my own advice, and
allowed the night sounds of the forest to fill my ears—the
peeps of the tree frogs and the murmurs of the crickets—
a sound that always reminded me of softly tearing cloth. I
listened as the noises seemed to magnify, blocking out the
rest of the world.

I sat straight up when a new din suddenly clamored in
the background. I strained to make out the cacophony—
the clanging sound of pots, the tinkle of bells, and the
laughing voices of men. Bells? Could it be Gracias, I wondered, angry over the death of his soldier? But there was
laughter and other noises that did not belong to Gracias.

"George," I whispered. "I'm going to join Henry to
see what all the commotion is about."

"Me, too," he said quickly. He obviously had not slept.

The two of us made our way through the brush to
crouch beside Henry, who was on his knees, pressed

against the trunk of a tree. He did not turn to look at us.

"They're getting close," he said. "And they don't care if the entire forest knows they're coming." He shook his head as if in disbelief. Whoever led their pack was carrying a torch. We watched its light bob with its bearer's footsteps. No soldier would enter an unknown territory in this way.

Soon we spied the shadowy forms of men and what appeared to be some animals in their wake—a few cows, some sheep or goats, and a cart laden with goods—most likely the source of the clanging sounds.

When they were just one hundred feet from us, I saw that the man carrying the torch used a walking stick. He used it to tap the cow beside him to keep the cow moving. He wore a multicolored tunic, good stockings, and fine leather boots. He had a generous stomach, which tipped over his belt, round cheeks, and a nose that looked red from the torchlight. His hair and beard blazed red, too. He appeared much too bright for this forest.

"Princess," the large red man suddenly yelled in a mock whisper. "The gravedigger told us that we would find you here."

"The merchants!" George yelped before I could cover his mouth.

"The gravedigger sent them," I barely whispered to Henry.

"But how do they know we are right here?" he said softly.

"Because I have a keen ear!" the man bellowed back to us. He stopped walking to adjust his belt. "And I have potions in my cart that can make your ears better than a dog's," he promised gleefully.

George began to stand. His eyes shone in the torchlight.

But Henry stood first and stepped into the road. His hand rested on the hilt of his sword. "Are you the merchants who are to guide us to Bordeaux?" Henry was squinting past the big man, as if trying to see what the rest of the merry band looked like.

"The very ones!" the colorful leader boasted. "Allow me to introduce myself and my four brothers. I am Albert the Round," he said, bowing. He rose and motioned for his brothers. They jockeyed around him, pushing aside Albert's cow. "Actually, we are all known as Albert, as it's less confusing for our customers," he said with a convincing smile, which exposed a few missing teeth. His brothers did look like variations of him—some taller, some thinner, and all in fine clothes, with hair the color of a snapping wood fire. "We feared we would not catch up to you, but now that we have, it is time to camp and eat. We will leave for Bordeaux at dawn," he added agreeably.

"And how are the other Alberts called?" George asked eagerly.

Henry cut him off. "You know that this is the princess and that she must be protected by you until we reach the city," Henry stated, without it even nearing the lilt of a question.

"Of course, my dear soldier. We were instructed by the gravedigger." Albert nodded. His brothers bobbed their heads in agreement on cue.

Henry sighed, unsure if he should be relieved by our new comrades. "We should try to be quiet, then, as we are being pursued," he added gravely.

"Indeed," Albert agreed. For a moment, the smile disappeared from his face.

"May I pet your cows and goats?" George interrupted eagerly, obviously thrilled with our new company.

Albert lifted his torch high above his head to get a good look at George. "Of course you may," he said. "After you help us set up our tent."

Albert kept his promise and had us up by dawn, although in the forest the morning light was a dusky rust, so that the trees, leaves, and human forms that moved about us all looked blurred around their edges. He handed George and me a mug of goat's milk as one of his brothers kicked at the campfire that they had built in our clearing. Henry was helping one brother pull the tent down, as the other brothers, their thick red hair and beards all in various states of dishevelment, made clicking sounds at their animals to gather them together. George and I sat on my sack of clothes as we sipped the warm, sweet milk.

Albert approached us, his full face still pressed with the lines of sleep. "We will be getting on now, princess. We should reach Bordeaux by sundown." He then took our empty mugs and placed them in a bucket of water on the cart.

"Of course," I said. "We are ready." George and I followed Albert to the cart that had been left on the edge of our clearing, only yards from the road. We did not have the opportunity to discover its contents last night.

"Chickens!" George exclaimed, as if they were a novelty. A wired cage in the cart contained six of them. All looked headless, as they were still slumbering beneath the shelter of their wings. I was more interested in the rows and rows of bottles of all sizes and colors. Each was marked with a name I could not read and sat in a crude tin pot, ready to catch its contents should the bottle break.

"Our potions," Albert said proudly. "We trade in remedies for all sorts of maladies, although Albert the Slim there," he said, pointing to the tall, thin brother with a pointy beard, "is yearning to learn alchemy." Slim Albert, hearing his name, wagged his finger at Round Albert. Obviously, this argument was an old one.

"Do you have a potion for the pestilence?" George asked, standing on tiptoe to reach the nearest bottle. Albert gently swatted him away.

"No, my dear boy. That is one curse that we have yet to find a pill, powder, or lotion for, but we will keep working on it."

Henry came up behind us. "Our horses are ready, Albert. Do you wish to lead the way?"

"Of course," he answered, his jovial nature seeming to awaken with the growing light. "I'm sure your horses will not mind the leisurely pace of the cows."

Indeed, the pace was slow. The steady gait of my horse and the coolness of the forest path, protected from the harshest glare of the sun, made me drowsy. I had to keep pinching myself to stay awake for fear I would fall off my horse and pull George along with me.

Albert and his brothers, two of them pulling their cart and the others constantly scampering after their animals, clogged the thin path in front of us. They talked incessantly, all at the same time, as if everything that they needed to say had to be said at this moment. Periodically, Albert would wave his walking stick at us as if he were leading a pageant. Henry rode quietly behind us, every so often turning his horse around to stare down the road we had recently traveled.

"May I walk with Albert, Nell?" George asked. "My rear is getting sore."

"It's princess," I whispered back, thinking that I would prefer to walk at this point, too.

I was ready to guide George out of the saddle when suddenly Henry's horse reared and thrashed his front hooves in the air. My horse bucked more gently, but his ears flicked back as he showed his teeth.

"What is it?" I yelled to Henry, but my question was drowned in a thundering boom and a flash of light that seemed to strike at some trees not far to the south of us. Another burst of light blazed in front of us, and I jumped in my saddle as George dug his fingernails into my waist.

Albert was using his walking stick now to swat at his brothers. "We must hurry!" he shouted. "I can smell a harsh storm. My brothers and I know of a cave not far from here." With that, the men and their menagerie began trotting up the road.

I turned back to Henry. *Why is he hesitating? Why is he not following us?* It was then that I saw it—a black stain, like a swarm of low-flying bees, moving toward us on the forest path. It moved steadily, heedless of the thunder and lightning erupting in the trees around us, and oblivious to the smell of metal and water that suddenly permeated the air. I moved my horse alongside Henry's and gripped him by the arm.

"The rats!" I yelled. "We must get to the cave." Although I did not know what we would do once we got there.

"Turn, Nell! Get in front of the merchants!" Henry shouted, anticipating the next crack of lightning. He grabbed at my horse's reins, not waiting for me to react as he turned his own horse around and pulled mine forward.

"What are we going to do?" George screamed as our horses trotted along the edge of the path, catching up to the procession and upsetting Albert's brothers and their animals. Only the cows wouldn't move to allow us to pass.

"What are they?" Albert puffed as he slowed to take another look behind us. He flinched as a searing light split a tree near the front line of the rats, which appeared to be gaining on us. Suddenly the huge tree, aflame, slammed across the forest path, cutting off their access.

"They are the Black Prince's rats!" I said, with what sounded like a wail to me, which only made me angry. "Are we near your cave?" I shouted.

"To the left, this way," Albert replied as he suddenly stopped to roll away a sizable stone from a tiny footpath. I glanced over my shoulder, and indeed, there was a rutted gully that had been carved into the steep hill on my left. From my vantage point, I could see an earthen mound, like a large boil, rising from the hill's summit. Its dome appeared and disappeared in the crowns of the storm-lashed trees. "Follow my brothers and take up your horses," Albert insisted. "There is room enough for us all!"

"Henry!" I called as my horse skittishly began climbing the winding, rock-gouged path to the cave. I looked over my shoulder to see him and his horse standing in the middle of the forest road, waiting.

It suddenly began to pour, a hard pelting rain that would easily extinguish any fire.

"He'll be coming, Nell. He's just waiting for us all to make it up this hillside," George reassured me. I shivered as the cold rain plastered my hair and clothes against my body.

Albert had managed to get to the top of the bluff before any of us and he stood at the entrance to a cave that yawned like a giant's mouth in the hillside. His wild red hair was flattened and his wet tunic, where it stretched across his belly, had a shine to it. He motioned frantically for us to hurry.

My horse made it to the top, and George and I quickly jumped off to assist the brothers with their goats and sheep. Henry was plodding behind the two cows, nearly shoving them up the hillside.

"Albert the Strong!" Albert yelled. "Don't forget our potions!" George and another red-haired brother ran out to help Strong Albert with his cart.

Finally we were all inside the cool, dank cave, peering past the curtain of rain to stare out at the tops of the trees that were being whipped around in the wind below us. The thunder and lightning continued unmercifully. Henry stood closest to the cave's mouth, his hand nervously clasping the hilt of his sword. It was a gesture I was coming to know all too well.

I turned to survey the cave where we were to hide like animals. It was amazingly wide—the span of a courtyard, with a high roof that provided ample headroom for even the horses. Just beyond the remnants of an old cooking fire, which blackened the center of the cave's floor, the ground pitched toward the back, to what looked like a hole. I could only discern its blackness.

The brothers all began talking again, raising their arms and scaring the livestock, which bucked and clucked around us. Albert stood by his cart, which the brothers had placed against the north wall, as if protecting it. Iron pegs had been rammed into the rock, and a worn brown cloak hung from each peg. Henry was whispering to our horses, which he had walked to the south wall of the cave. He was rubbing their noses soothingly as they looked around the cave, wide-eyed. George covered his ears with his hands in the ruckus. The brothers were all yelling about the rats, about why they were coming after us.

"Are you cursed, princess?" Albert attempted to ask politely, his one hand nervously stroking his beard as his other latched onto his belt.

I looked around at his sodden circle of brothers, all their earlier cheer gone as they waited for my reply. I am a nobody, I wanted to reply, whose worth is only in what she pretends to be.

"I am afraid I am," I said, a horrid feeling of guilt washing over me. *What have I gotten these innocent people into?* "The Black Prince has set these rats on us, because he wants me back." *Is the Black Prince near?* With the thought, I felt the heat drain from my face.

"Well, he will not have you, though!" Henry interrupted. His eyes suddenly seemed to reflect the burdens of an older man. "Albert, can you and your brothers make a quick fire?" he asked.

"Indeed we can!" Albert answered excitedly, as if glad to have a call to action. "Our tinder is in the far corner there!" he reminded a brother, pointing into the darkness of the cave, far from the hole. Two of the brothers clambered into the blackness, until they could be seen only as shadows.

"Our situation reminds me of the trial of a great Greek who battled his own monster in a cave long ago. We should call upon him for inspiration," Albert proclaimed.

"What about your potions, Albert?" I asked, truly inspired by his bravery. George ran over to the cart to peer in. "Do any of them repel rats?"

Albert scratched his beard. "Not that I recall," he said. "Although I never really tried to concoct a potion for that purpose."

George already had his hand around the throat of one of the shiny red bottles. "Perhaps we can just try a few, then?" he asked hopefully.

Albert frowned but before he could reply, Henry shouted, "The rats! They are coming up the hill!"

I pushed my way forward to stand beside him. Sure enough, a shimmering black line began to snake its way up the hillside.

"Bring up the fire!" Henry called.

"And the potions!" I added. "We can make a fire wall outside of the entrance. Hurry!"

Immediately, Albert, George, and Strong and Slim Albert pulled stoppers out of bottles and poured them in a half circle extending out from our cave. The other two brothers—Albert the Red and Albert the Shy—were right behind them. Each held a flaming torch in hand, which they touched to the potion-saturated ground before the rain snuffed out their flames.

A barrier of fire shot up, wavering and then roaring back to life despite the driving storm. The dirty black smoke barely masked the rows of beady eyes and twitching noses that crouched on the other side of our barricade of fire. There must have been a hundred rats, their soaked bodies trembling impatiently at the rain and at our fire.

I prayed that if the fire did not keep them back, perhaps the sickly sweet, stinging aroma of the burning potions would. But the rats appeared undeterred as they stared oblivious to the fire and rain that raged around us. I heard Albert and his brothers collectively gasp as a section of our fire wall wilted for a moment, pounded by a surging gust of wind. We all knew that our blockade would not last much longer.

"What is in the back of the cave?" I asked desperately. I thought of the hole. I was hoping for a means of escape.

"Nothing but a hole, princess. A hole that burrows deep into the earth," Albert said, shaking his head. He put his arm around his smallest brother, Albert the Shy, a brother more freckled than the rest.

"You've stuck your head in that cavity many times, Shy Albert," he said, as if speaking to a child. "What did you see? I know it's as least as round as my waist," Albert added, patting his stomach affectionately.

Shy Albert attempted to wipe his face dry as he looked down at his boots. "It was very cold in the hole and it smelled like damp earth," he replied. "Its blackness showed no bottom to it."

"How about the rats?" I asked. Henry's eyes met mine as the same thought charged between us.

"You do have more potions?" Henry suggested. "We need to create two lines of fire, lines that will form a single pathway for them, from the cave entrance to the hole."

Albert's eyes widened. "We do," he acknowledged, although he glanced at his remaining potions as if they were treasures he could not easily part with. His brothers gathered around him and again they all began arguing at once. Behind them, I could see George already standing on his toes, leaning into the cart.

Albert wheeled around. "Boy!" he yelled, his face contorted as if in pain. "Grab those potions and begin pouring."

Again we unstopped the thin, delicate bottles and started to pour two parallel lines from the fire wall that rimmed our cave's mouth to the mysterious dark hole. Henry grabbed one of the brother's cloaks and approached the mass of living fur. Some of them began snarling, at Henry or the fire, tired of this game.

The torches were relit and their bearers touched their fire to the fresh trails of potions. The aisle to the hole whooshed to life. Inside the cave, the heat was smothering.

"Run to the hole, all of you!" Henry urged. "They will track you there."

As we all gathered on the other side of the hole, we stared down the center of the fire walk. I clung to George, who seemed intent on looking into the abyss. He kicked a rock into the hole. It hit one side and then fell. We never heard the impact.

"Be ready!" Henry yelled as he used the cloak to extinguish a segment of the flames that intercepted our aisle. The rats were leaping over one another now, snapping at their brethren in front of them in their frenzy. In a moment, their entry into the cave was no longer guarded. Henry pulled the cloak away as waves of the vile creatures suddenly charged down the aisle, right toward us.

I wanted to scream as the rodent army hurtled toward the hole, seemingly insensible to the fire that hemmed them in on both sides. We stood mesmerized, as whole packs of them poured into the chasm, the seemingly endless hole that swallowed up every last rat. They squealed as they fell, their cries echoing off of the cave's walls, creating a nightmarish sound. We never heard them hit the ground.

Within a minute they were gone and their screeches were replaced by the softer rumblings of thunder moving off into the distance. Wordlessly, we each picked up a cloak or a blanket and began to beat down the flames in the cave. Coughing was a relief, as it signified that we were still alive. Finally I looked at Henry, who had his back now to the cave's entrance. Behind him stood a hooded figure.

"Good show," Gracias said, shaking his head and causing his bells to jingle. "I couldn't have done better myself."

the potion

ALBERT WAS THE FIRST to speak, although Henry had been the first to act. As the brothers and I stared stupidly at the minstrel blocking our cave, Henry whirled around as he pulled his sword from his belt and held its hilt with both hands. He muttered and lowered his sword when he saw it was Gracias.

"And who are you?" Albert asked in wonder. Thunderous black clouds appeared to rest on the shoulders of the black-bearded minstrel in the multicolored tunic with bells. Truly, his towering image was a fearsome one. Albert's brothers closed around him. Albert the Slim grasped George and pulled him close.

But George pushed away. "It's Gracias!" he announced,

as if relieved. "He helped us escape the Black Prince," he added proudly.

"Please, do come in," Albert invited, as if this smoke-filled cave that stung our nostrils with its acrid potion smells were his proud home.

Gracias laughed and, after a theatrical bow, entered. It was then that I realized what a perfect disguise a minstrel's costume was, for how could anyone initially fear a man, even a large man, who jingled as he walked and talked. But I was still unsure if we could trust him.

I introduced the brothers and Gracias, and quickly attempted to bring Gracias up to date on the events that took place since he had left us. *What harm is there in this telling?* It certainly could not change what had passed.

Gracias nodded solemnly when I finished. "I know who killed my *soldados*," he said bitterly. "We had been following your *Príncipe Negro*, your Black Prince, since we left you. *El cobarde*, the coward crept upon our camp in the darkness of night like an animal," he sneered, his bushy black eyebrows gathering in a frown. "One of my soldados was killed immediately and I sent the one who survived after you, to warn you that your prince was close in pursuit." Gracias paused and clenched his fists before continuing. "I chased the prince but he had vanished like a *espíritu maligno*."

Albert, George, and the brothers listened to Gracias's story with their mouths open. Henry stared at Gracias, his gaze searching the minstrel's face for a fault. Gracias turned his head to return the look.

"How did the rats find you again?" he asked, bending toward Henry mockingly. "Did you summon them somehow?"

Henry stepped back, looking more shocked than outraged. "I don't know what you mean, sir," he said. His body trembled.

"Really," Gracias drawled, his eyes never leaving Henry's pained face. "Sir Andrew told me that you were employed to track the princess at all costs. Who are you tracking her for, soldado? Sir Andrew or the prince?"

"That is ridiculous!" I interrupted. George's eyes were wide as Albert and his brothers stepped away from us, as if sensing another attack. "Henry has done nothing but protect us," I protested. "Let him be."

Henry said nothing, until he raised his eyes again, almost pleadingly as he looked into my face.

"The Black Prince talked to me about chivalry," Henry said. His tone sounded betrayed. "The prince told me to keep you safe and not to let you out of my sight." He looked away from me.

"Is that why you are with us now?" I demanded to know. My throat tightened. I feared I might cry. I wondered if this was the reason he cast so many dark glances Gracias's way.

"No," he answered fiercely. "At first yes, but not now. A legion of rats from hell is not chivalrous. Marrying you falsely is not chivalrous. Killing those who are also seeking to protect you is not chivalrous! This is not the way of our king!" He looked us all in the eye now. He was still trembling, but with rage instead of shame.

"Then why are the rats following you, soldado? How do they know how to find you?" Gracias prodded, his chin defiantly in the air.

"I don't know," Henry answered. "On my honor."

"I know how," George's small voice interrupted. We all turned to look at him, pressed against the line of brothers. He pulled the amulet from around his neck, the amulet that Henry had buried in the gravedigger's woods. I shook my head at his dirty arms. Why hadn't I realized what he had done earlier?

"Oh, George," was all that I could say.

We spent the night in the cave. Gracias insisted that we remain there. He was sure that any surviving rats would smell the death of their brothers that came before them and stay away. He also took George's amulet as he readied to mount his horse, extending his huge hand in a command. Despite his bells and colorful tunic, there was nothing comical about Gracias. When he wasn't smiling, his thick black eyebrows and beard made him appear all the more severe. George tentatively left the safety of the cave as he dropped the amulet in Gracias's outstretched hand.

Gracias rubbed the amulet between his thumb and forefinger and frowned, his eyebrows intersecting in a *V*.

"You, senor. Give me one of your *pociónes*," he called. Albert suddenly scurried from the cave, clutching a green-colored bottle by its long, thin neck.

"Grab a stick, boy, and allow the amulet to rest on it as this gentleman pours his liquid."

George carefully edged to the toe of the bluff to pick up a stick. Albert watched in silence as George returned to hold the amulet by the stick's tip. It dangled on its thin chain.

"Pour, senor," Gracias instructed.

Lines of sweat appeared on Albert's forehead, yet his hand remained steady as he slowly poured the contents of the bottle over the amulet. A hissing steam rose from the metal.

"Ahh," Gracias said as he took the stick from George. Albert, George, and I leaned in closer to peer at the amulet. I could just barely make out the strange words scratched into the amulet's back.

"What does it say?" I asked in dread.

"It's an incantation," Gracias replied.

"But my amulet didn't have those marks," George protested.

"Then perhaps this amulet belonged to the príncipe. Did he show you one?" Gracias prodded, gently now.

"Yes!" George answered excitedly. "He said that our matching amulets made us like brothers."

Gracias smiled knowingly. "He switched them. This amulet has served as his hawk. It has been tracking you like prey."

The image of the Black Prince proudly holding his amulet next to George's suddenly came to my mind. It was after George shared his lunch with the two little French girls. I recalled that despite his feigned friendship with George, my heart had recoiled at the menace in his eyes. An incantation. A curse. Were those similar spells he offered as he danced around the fires on the beach of Bordeaux?

"You won't dare dig it up again, will you, boy?" Gracias asked severely, interrupting my thoughts. He slipped the amulet into a pocket in his tunic.

George shook his head while looking at his feet. Albert nodded gravely, as if he, too, were making a pledge.

I looked beyond Gracias, at the black forms of the treetops below us that seemed pressed into the night sky. There were no stars or moon tonight. The thunderclouds, though silent now, smothered them all.

"When will you be back?" I asked him. I shivered, thinking of us all sleeping in this cave.

He turned to follow my line of sight and then looked back at me. His teeth, exposed in a teasing smile, seemed to glow eerily in the blackness like an animal's.

"I will be back by dawn," he said. "Then we will get on with the final part of your *viaje* to Bordeaux."

It was then that I felt Henry's presence behind me.

"I will be with you," he pledged in my ear.

I nodded, but did not turn to look into his eyes. When I felt him walk away, I attempted a smile at George and Albert.

"We all should get some sleep," I advised.

Albert agreed. "I am going to instruct my brothers to lay out their blankets by the cart. We have enough to share with you, princess, and for your two soldiers."

George perked up at that. "I will lay them out," he

volunteered. Without waiting for an answer, he ran back into the cave to the knot of Albert's brothers.

We rested by the cart as Henry took the first watch by the cave's entrance. I watched him tether our horses to a tree, only feet away from our shelter. They both began to tear at the leaves that dangled before their eyes. I then picked up my blanket as Henry threw his cloak over his shoulders and squatted, his back to us, as he gazed into the night.

I shivered beneath my own cloak, as I pulled George's over his shoulders as he slept beside me. The bulky forms of Albert and his brothers were lined along the wall of the cave, far from the hole that led to the other side of the earth. I listened to their snoring, trying to take comfort in their faith that it was safe to sleep. Their collection of animals, clustered around them, made their own night noises, and lent an earthy smell to our potion-filled cave. Only the cows remained standing, their eyelids closed, as if that was all that was needed to escape the world.

Henry. George and I needed Henry, despite the things that Gracias made him confess. I would have to trust that his heart was pure, as I felt that, if not, my own would break. How I despised the night, I realized, as it brought such black thoughts.

These were the worries that folded into my sleep. I held George's hand as I held the image of Henry, guarding the cave entrance, in my head. But my bitterness towards the prince soon pressed against my dreams, which became filled with the angry squeals of rats.

A yelp from Albert the Shy awoke me. Shy Albert had been on watch when Gracias returned and the sight of the minstrel's companion was the cause of Shy Albert's alarm.

It was the gravedigger.

He stood beside Gracias at the mouth of the cave. In the early morning mist that seemed to hang like a tapestry woven from otherworldly threads, the two figures did indeed appear like ghosts.

I arose slowly, pulling my cloak around my shoulders. Henry was already standing, squinting at the spectral forms. The air smelled of dew and sweat and spoiling potions. The snores of Albert and his other brothers reverberated softly within the confines of the cave.

"Gracias?" I whispered, not wanting to wake George and Albert and his brothers. "Is that the gravedigger?"

"The very same," the gravedigger replied eagerly amidst the vapor. "I'm so glad to see that you are safe, princess. I knew that Albert could protect you."

Henry joined me as I approached the cave entrance. Shy Albert cut between us, seeking the comfort of his sleeping brothers.

Indeed, there stood the gravedigger, next to a smiling Gracias. His gray beard was beaded with dew and his blue eyes were clear as glass. If at all possible, his brown tunic and red stockings were even dirtier than when I last saw him standing among the death pits. I flinched for a moment, imagining a long succession of burials since yesterday.

"Thank you for sending Albert, sir." I almost curtsied but stopped myself. I never saw the princess curtsy to anyone save the king, much less a gravedigger, but I was so pleased to see another friendly face. "He and his brothers have been most helpful to us. Will you be joining us now?" I asked a bit hopefully.

At this, the gravedigger scratched his thick black hair and looked at Gracias. The snoring brothers dispelled any possibility of a thoughtful silence. And then Gracias shook his head, his bell tinkling softly.

"The gravedigger will be your *último* and only guide to Bordeaux, princesa. You shall arrive as so many have already left," Gracias said, his amused smile conveying no doubt as to his meaning.

"You aren't serious?" Henry interjected. "Should we really mock death in such a manner?"

The gravedigger reached out now, startling Henry by placing his dirty, weathered hand on Henry's shoulder.

"The dead cannot be mocked, monsieur. It is they who mock the living. Do not worry about their *honneur*," the gravedigger admonished. "They are not burdened by such vices."

"Surely there must be another way," Henry insisted. He glanced at me, as if waiting for me to back him up.

"There is not," Gracias replied dismissively. "Unless you know something that we do not, that might lend itself to an alternate plan?" Gracias raised his thick black eyebrows. His sardonic smile implied his meaning.

Henry's blue eyes flashed. His fists were balled. "You do trust me, don't you, princess? You don't believe the insinuations of this sly heathen, do you?" he asked desperately.

I did not like what Gracias was proposing any more than Henry, but I knew we had no other choice but to trust Gracias's allegiance to us. Had he not had many opportunities to give us up to the prince, or to do away with us himself? And it did appear, from what we knew or could deduce, that the Black Prince considered Gracias an enemy.

I stared hard at our little circle that contained the mocking minstrel, a chastened soldier, and an oddly serene gravedigger. With the exception of the gravedigger, suspicion was our strongest link. I knew then that to survive, I would need to cut that thread.

"We would be honored to share you as our guide, sir," I said, ignoring the fear in Henry's eyes. I would need to be brave enough for us all.

Only Albert was bold enough to bid us farewell on the forest path. It was just after dawn and last night's thunderous clouds still filled the sky. His dark cloak muted his usually bright attire but his red hair and beard served as a beacon for his brothers, who were gathered together in a clump on the top of the hill, peering down at us anxiously.

Henry had offered to go first, to show George that there was really no harm in being wrapped like the dead. I felt a rush of warmth for Henry, as I knew the terror the death carts held for him. He had told me of the nightmares, which visited him still, where he is a young boy again, working with the men who pulled the carts through the streets of London during its last great plague. He told me that in each dream, the bodies are piled higher than a haystack, until he can no longer pull the cart beneath such weight. In his dream, the bodies begin to mock him. They call him names and laugh, turning their heads to stare at him with wide black mouths full of worms. He stood there now allowing Gracias to approach him, for whom he held no regard. I wanted to grab his hands and thank him, but instead I offered my gratitude through a smile.

He noticed but looked away, almost shyly, as he stood beside the gravedigger's death cart as Gracias dropped the dirty white shroud over his head and wrapped it around his body.

"I will not be able to move," Henry growled from within. Albert hugged George as he gasped.

"That is Henry talking, George, not a ghost," I said gently as Albert and George stared fish-eyed as Gracias picked Henry up like a small boy and laid him full length in the bottom of the wooden cart. He then placed Henry's sword, blade down, beside him.

"You are not supposed to move, soldado. You are *muerto*. Remember that, or the game will be up," Gracias replied severely. He glanced at me as if sensing my stare. "You need to trust us, princesa," he said, seeing all the fear on my face. I tried to dismiss the image of my father and my mother the last time I saw them. They had been tossed into a cart, not very different from this one, like rank garbage. This was the impression that had stayed with me since their deaths. The pestilence had robbed them of their lives and stole from me any comforting memories.

"I will go next," George suddenly volunteered, breaking away from Albert in a burst of bravery. "I trust you, Gracias, and the gravedigger, too." His stocking-covered knees were trembling violently, though.

"*Muchacho bueno*," Gracias said, not seeming to notice, or at least pretending not to. He lifted George into the cart and swaddled him in the death wraps. I immediately went over to him to hold his hand for as long as I could. I knew that George was being brave for me.

"When can we expect to arrive?" Henry barked, shimmying aside to make room for George.

"Perhaps by late afternoon," the gravedigger responded. "I travel the forest paths gently, and no living man purposely gets in my way. You should all take a *petit somme*, a good nap," he encouraged. His blue eyes looked soft in the fading darkness. The birds of the forest trilled, as if in agreement.

"Princess," Albert reached out to me, pulling from the pocket of his cloak a red bottle in the shape of a long thin vial about the length of my hand. A potion.

"The *garçon* asked me if I had a potion for rats. I did not before, but I mixed a few together last night. It is a mixture that I hope can address all the creatures of the dark. Hold on to this," he finished, slipping it into my cloak pocket.

Again I did not curtsy, though I wanted so badly to hug Albert, as if he were my father. I extended my hand instead, as I knew the real princess would have done, but my eyes, unlike hers ever did, blurred with tears as Albert stooped and kissed my hand gently.

I turned awkwardly to Gracias.

"I am ready," I said.

betrayal

I TRIED TO SLEEP, but of course it was impossible. The bindings were tight and made any real movement impossible and if I took too deep a breath, it felt as if a gloved hand covered my mouth and nose. The best I could do was rock my body to keep it from going numb. I did not know what thoughts went through Henry's head as he lay beside me in the cart, dressed in the death wrappings, but I prayed that his nightmares were kept at bay by my presence. I knew that courage was often born when one needed to be brave for others. I told myself that I needed to summon my own courage, too, as I felt George trembling against my side. *Does he relive that day in London in his dreams, too?*

"I am here, George," I mumbled through the shroud.

"Why don't you go to sleep?"

I was thankful when eventually he did.

My own thoughts were fed by a porridge of feelings. We did not talk, as Gracias had insisted. We knew that such idle chatter could be the death of us. Instead I mentally reviewed our conversation beside the death cart. Henry and I had peppered Gracias with a few more questions.

"What if some family along our way wishes to add a body to the cart?"

Gracias said that the gravedigger would know what to do. Besides, he added, almost anyone left in the forest villages between here and Bordeaux had already died if they were meant to do so. Also, Gracias had warned us that we would have to exit the cart before we reached the gates into Bordeaux, as a death cart entering the city at this time would appear highly suspicious.

I had run through a number of scenarios as I listened to the gravedigger hum his haunting tunes. When he wasn't humming, or addressing the birds, as he was wont to do, I tried to concentrate on taking note of the daytime sounds of the forest that mingled with our squeaking cartwheel, which was jarring yet soothingly rhythmic at the same time. I listened to the birds, the cicadas, a distant howl—the sounds of life around us seemingly unaffected by men. I was glad to have such sounds, anything to keep out the thoughts of the past or of my immediate future.

But such daydreams only sufficed for some time.

Soon we would arrive in Bordeaux, and according to Gracias, give ourselves over to the protection of its mayor. *Will he send us back to England to tell the king what happened? Will the king believe me?* The Black Prince was his blood. I was nothing but a servant.

Or will the mayor hide us in Bordeaux to ensure that my marriage to the prince of Castile does not take place? Neither choice consoled me.

I suddenly began to panic.

"Princess," Henry whispered in my ear. "You are breathing much too quickly. Are you all right?" Henry sounded as anxious as me.

"I do not know if this is right for us, Henry. What will happen to us in Bordeaux?" I tried to keep my voice even.

"Well, this is a fine time to have second thoughts," he muttered, "with us wrapped like pickled fish."

"You didn't have any other ideas," I replied accusingly, angry with him now for not comforting me.

"*You* are the princess, and you seem to favor Gracias's

advice," he shot back as best as he could through the muzzle of cloth. "I am nothing but a soldier."

I am *not* the princess I wanted to scream, but held my tongue. I attempted to inch away from him, but George's sleeping body wedged me in.

The cart suddenly dropped to a halt. "The dead I carry are usually not so talkative," the gravedigger said, without a hint of sarcasm. It was hard to tell if he was angry without seeing his face. I felt ashamed. We should not have talked so freely. We did not know how much Gracias had told the gravedigger. I was not behaving like the princess.

Neither Henry nor I said a word.

George jolted awake, though, at the abrupt end of the cart's lulling motion.

"Are we there, Nell?" he asked, his voice high as a tiny child's.

I hoped the gravedigger did not hear him, but how could I be angry with George when I had behaved badly?

"Not yet, garçon," the gravedigger answered. "We have just a bit longer to go. Should I continue?" he asked. I could feel the cart being lifted by its handles.

"Yes," I said. "It is not you I question, sir," I added contritely.

"I know that, princess," he answered warmly. "But you have no need to fear. The mayor is a good man."

The gravedigger stopped again at the end of the forest, where its wildflower fields spilled out to the gatehouse of the walled city. He had hidden the cart in a small grove of trees, young trees whose leaves were still soft like babies' skin and whose height rose barely two feet above Henry's head. He lifted us out one by one—first myself, then George, and finally Henry. We each inhaled deeply and tasted the earth as our shrouds dropped away. We needed that breath, because once our eyes became accustomed to the blinding sunlight, we gasped again at our first sight of Bordeaux. We clung to the sapling branches as we peered at the fortress before us.

"It suffered much," the gravedigger said, as if reading our thoughts. "First by the Black Death, and then by the fires. The mayor did not mean for so much to burn."

I grabbed George's hand. Henry stood close by my side, our afternoon disagreement obviously forgotten. A breeze smelling of the sea touched our faces. Its salt caused my stomach to stir. I realized we had not eaten since yesterday morning.

Two soldiers stood by the first gatehouse that gave entry to the lower city. Bordeaux filled the entire horizon like a monstrous hearth fire that had been stamped out and forgotten. Its walls were blackened, as were the walls of the castle that rose over the city like its once majestic crown. The grand capital was nothing more than ashes.

From our lush grove, which seemed oblivious to the devastation before us, we could spy beyond the city's walls and stare at piles of rubble and scorched timber—all that was left of the peasants' housing. Only a stone church appeared to have survived unscathed with the exception of patches of burned thatch in its roof. A grove of trees by the moat was nothing but blackened stumps. I clung more fiercely to the living branches surrounding us.

On the other side of the moat, the castle's walls were intact, as were the walls of the corner towers. The metal grille of the gatehouse leading to the castle was closed, protecting it from its own people. The castle's keep, where I guessed the mayor must be, was also charred.

"I don't see any people besides those two soldiers," George pointed out.

He was right. There were no soldiers pacing along the wall walks, nor did there appear to be anyone entering or leaving the city.

"What does this mean?" I asked the gravedigger. I felt my heart in my throat.

He shrugged. "That my work in Bordeaux is finished, but yours, princess, is just beginning."

We had no choice but to approach the soldiers if we wanted to reach the mayor. The gravedigger waited with his cart at the forest's fringe. I held George's small, sweaty hand as the three of us walked across the empty expanse of land between the wildflower field and the gatehouse, covered now with nothing but sun-baked dust.

"I don't like the look of this," Henry confided as we neared the gatehouse. The two soldiers, one tall and thin, the other older and hunched, shielded their eyes with their hands as they kept their watch on us.

"Please, Henry, that doesn't help," I said as I felt George's grip tighten. I checked an urge to pull my cloak more tightly around me.

"Princess," the older soldier greeted as they both dropped to their knees. "We are happy to see that you are safe." He looked up at me, his squinting eyes almost lost in his pockmarked face. His brown tunic was dirty and he had rents in his stocking's at both knees. His armored vest was rusted and his helmet was dented. The young, thin soldier looked no better.

I nodded, not wanting to say anything. George had released my hand and cocked his head, sharing my thoughts. The king's soldiers in Windsor would never appear so shabby. I prayed that he knew better than to say anything.

But it was Henry who spoke. "Where is the remainder of the army?" he asked, looking at the castle's empty walls. "We did not all go with the prince." His hands were on his hips, as if he were their commander and deserved an answer.

The young soldier scowled, making his face look hawk-like. "Many died. Others fled while the town burned. The flames did not respect the castle." There was more than a little sarcasm in his voice

"We will take you to the mayor now," the old soldier interrupted gruffly. He swatted the other on the shoulder as he motioned for the younger to begin turning the crank. The iron gate began to rise slowly, emitting a horrible squeal. The tortuous work of the metal reminded me of the frustrated cries of the rats. *The Black Prince. Where is he now?* Hopefully, days away in the forest behind us.

When the portcullis was halfway up, the old soldier indicated for us to duck under and follow him into the city. The young soldier was to wait behind to lower the gate again.

The three of us were quiet as we followed the soldier

past the burned shells of houses. The air smelled like moldy ashes and a loose shutter banged in the wind. Did everyone die from the pestilence? Or were they chased away by the fires? If they were still alive, would they ever come back? It saddened me to think that a city could be orphaned, too.

I kept my sights on Bordeaux's cobbled street, as the roadway to the castle wall was all that looked normal. The city walls seemed to be closing in on us, as if pulling us into their lonely, desperate embrace.

As we crossed the drawbridge and its fetid moat, I fought a rising panic. *What will the mayor have us do? What plans does he have for us?* I felt my own palms begin to sweat. I was giving us up to this man who I sensed I could trust. I could still see the anguish in his dark eyes when we first met, but really, I knew nothing about him. *But what choice do I have?*

Henry glanced at me as if he sensed my thoughts. He gave me a smile, as if trying to assure me that all would be well.

The spiked portcullis to the castle was raised as we approached and I could see more soldiers inside the castle's walls. Some bowed, others glanced away nervously, as we passed them. They stood with sword or bow in hand, as if guarding the well or the stables, but it did not appear as if there was anyone to guard against. *Only us*, I thought, closing my fists tightly to cease the tremors.

One soldier made the sign of the cross as he passed in front of the chapel that hugged the embankment of the keep. I did not want to interpret their behavior, fearing that it would only raise my anxiety. Instead I thought about the last time we had entered this courtyard. We had come from the port side, and my largest worry then was what it would be like for us to live in Castile. How far we had come in such a short time.

From this approach, from the city wall, the castle's keep seemed all the more foreboding. The yellowed stone of its rounded walls was charred, yet the flag of the Plantagenets still fluttered from its pointed black roof. The shadowed arrow loops of the keep stared at us, reminding me of the eye slits in a warrior knight's helmet. *From which hole does he peer at the enemy whose death was imminent?* One never could tell. Yet it was the flag that made my heart pause, although I reasoned that the mayor would certainly not attempt to reclaim the castle from England on his own.

The soldier banged hard on the thick wooden door before we entered. He grunted as he pushed it open. I thought I heard George take a gulp of air.

My chest tightened as we ascended the spiral stone staircase. We passed the level of the keep's living quarters, where the princess had rested so briefly before this plague claimed her. We climbed the stairs to the next level, to the room that was reserved for the king or the Black Prince. The prince. My heart seized. I tried to ignore thoughts of the dungeon below, with its trapdoor leading to the pits. Were those rats that the Black Prince had so gleefully showed me the same rats that had pursued us to Albert's cave? I hoped so. We should never have to worry about *those* rats again.

We reached the floor of the king's quarters. Torches blazed on the walls surrounding us. A soldier stood on either side of the door that led to its inner chambers.

The room appeared empty.

Our soldier rapped against the door with his fist and then opened it slowly.

"The mayor regrets that he is a bit behind time, princess. But he asked that I make sure that you are all comfortable," the old soldier said, addressing his boots.

The torches cast dancing shadows on the walls of the dimly lit room. A thick wooden table with four cushioned chairs stood on its far side. Pewter cups and bowls were set at each place. Steaming plates rested at its center. My stomach seemed to leap at the mixed aroma of rabbit and goose. I heard George's stomach grumble with my own.

"The mayor insists that you do not wait for him," the soldier said, as no one took a step. "We will have fresh clothes for you all once you have eaten."

Nothing appeared to be amiss as I quickly surveyed the darker corners of the room. "Thank you, sir," I said. "We will dine as we await the mayor."

He nodded brusquely and turned quickly to the door. I jumped as it slammed behind us with such force that the torch fires shivered.

"I don't like this place," George whispered in a tiny voice. "It's much too quiet."

Henry walked cautiously to the table. "I'm with George. Something doesn't feel right." But he was eyeing the food with the look of a starving man.

"Come, let us eat. We are all faint from a lack of nourishment. Perhaps once we eat, our spirits will calm," I tried to reassure us.

We each took a place at the table. In addition to the rabbit and goose, there were plates of cabbage and turnips and a loaf of white bread. Our cups were filled with wine.

We ate in silence with the appetites of the hunters in

the tapestries on the wall overlooking our table. The hunters stood by their horses, triumphantly holding up their prey. Arrows had pierced the breasts of both animal and fowl in their possession. I tried to ignore their vacant, lifeless stares.

Henry was the first to push away from the table. "Princess, I don't believe I have ever eaten so well." He patted his stomach to show that it was full.

George nodded in agreement and gave me a grease-coated smile.

It was then that we were interrupted by a soft knock at the door.

I stood up. My heart began to beat ferociously. *Are my nerves to be so useless for the rest of my life?* I could barely hear my own voice as I said, "Sir de Bisquale, we must thank you for your kindness."

But Henry grabbed my arm to stop me as the cloaked figure entered the room.

It was the Black Prince.

"I missed you, sister," he said with a mocking smile.

I must have looked like I was gazing upon a specter because the prince only laughed as he looked into my face.

"Where is the mayor?" I asked, insanely, knowing it didn't make a difference.

"Put your sword down, soldier," the Black Prince said past me, "before I have my men cut the boy in half."

I turned to see Henry lowering his sword, as two new soldiers rushed into the room to grab George. They lifted him from the ground as he kicked and swung at them. "Let me go!" he shouted.

The prince replied with a serene smile, "To answer your question, princess, the mayor has been called away, as mayors sometimes are. I offered to welcome you in his place."

"It won't work," I said, searching his face for a shred of humanity. "I can't be the princess. Everyone could tell just by looking at me. It could have caused war . . . " I reasoned desperately.

"Shh. I know, I know," he said softly, as if wanting to give me comfort. "Nothing we can do about that now. My mistake." He bowed. "Your mistake was living long enough to meet up with me again." The corners of his mouth rose slowly as he straightened.

Suddenly the door crashed wide open, as four more soldiers entered the room.

"Take the soldier and the brat to the dungeon," the prince ordered, satisfaction laced in his voice.

"No!" I screamed as the soldiers struggled with

George and Henry. The two who already held George grabbed him by his waist and legs to cart him away. The others contented themselves with pummeling Henry as he attempted to raise his sword and fight them off. He was no match for the six.

"Yes, I still have legions of them," the Black Prince purred, as if reading my fear.

My mind raced as I listened to George calling my name as the soldiers dragged them out the door. I could hear Henry's curses as the soldiers began to descend the stairs.

"Come here, sister," the prince hissed. "I missed you."

He stepped towards the table. I saw the flash of a dagger in his hand before he slipped it into a pocket of his black cloak. *He is going to kill me.*

I looked around the room as he drew closer. He scurried like an animal, ready to spring. I needed a weapon. I tried to concentrate despite my pounding heart. The torches? The fire poker?

And then I remembered the potion that Albert had given me—in a flask in the pocket of my cloak. My hand felt its smooth coolness. My thumb searched for its stopper.

I threw the flask's contents at him as he lunged at me. The yellow liquid splattered in the prince's face. Beads of the liquid clung to his eyelashes and beard. I had never seen these emotions—a mixture of shock and fear—grace his face before.

He screamed in pain as his hair and cloak began smoking. He covered his face with his hands as he hurtled his body against the table and fell to the floor.

I was frozen to the spot, appalled by the sight, until I heard George scream my name again. He already sounded far away.

I bolted from the room and charged down the spiral stairs. The prince's screams echoed off the walls around me.

The soldiers had paused on the last flight of stairs and were staring up with their mouths open. Even George and Henry had quieted.

"Run!" I yelled at them. "The prince has the pestilence!" The soldiers looked at me, dazed, their expressions slack.

"Can't you hear his screams?" I insisted.

The soldiers knew what to do. The ravage of this plague was still fresh on their minds. They dropped George and released Henry, who slumped to the floor. His face was badly beaten.

"Help me, George. We must get to the docks."

George's blue eyes widened. "Where are we going?" he asked.

"Anywhere! To any boat that will take us. We must get out of Bordeaux!" I did not care where we went. I just wanted us away from the prince.

"The docks are too far for Henry to go," George cried. He scrambled behind Henry to lift him by his armpits.

"Pull me up, George. That's it. Once I'm up, I'll be able to manage," he insisted. His voice sounded almost normal. I worried that he might be stunned, but he reached for his discarded sword as George and I both heaved him to his feet.

The fleeing soldiers had left the door of the keep open and I caught a strong scent of the sea, which heartened me. I could see the dock in my mind—through the courtyard, past the well and the servants' quarters—a run that would take us at least two hundred yards before we reached the gatehouse that opened to the cliff that overlooked the ocean. I could see the path perfectly, as each detail had been seared in my memory when we arrived in Bordeaux. The stone stairs carved into the cliff numbered fifty. If needed, we would tumble down them, as long as we reached the dock. They were a straight drop, without the bends and curves reserved for the faint of heart.

Henry's first steps were more of a swagger, but as we made our way through the courtyard, his gait acquired the stoicism reserved for battle. George straightened, too, and looked fierce. When some puzzled soldiers approached us and hesitated, they raised their swords halfheartedly. Those that were bolder backed away quickly when I yelled with all the hysteria I could muster, "The prince has the pestilence!"

We were passing the kitchen when the two young soldiers who were guarding the gatehouse reached for their swords. The keep's blacksmith slammed the shutter of his workroom as we approached. I heard George whisper conspiratorially, "I can help you get better, Henry, once we stop running." Henry scowled, or looked to be scowling, as both his eyes were turning purple and puffy.

I suddenly felt a fierce love for both of them that must have made my eyes seem to blaze, for the gatehouse soldiers stepped back.

Henry planted both feet firmly on the ground, as if to support the weight of the sword he slowly raised. The skeptical young soldiers, who were blocking our path through the already-raised portcullis, eyed Henry and then me, as George suddenly ordered, "Let the princess pass!"

They looked at each other, and then back at Henry and me—a princess running away from a betrothal and a soldier who appeared beaten and crazed from battle.

"Do as he says," I commanded imperiously. "I wish to get to my ship."

They almost had stepped aside, their mouths pinched in confusion, until one suddenly tugged on the other's sleeve.

"Is that the Black Prince?" the one with the deeper voice croaked.

I turned to look back toward the castle and silenced a scream in my throat. Indeed, it was the prince. He was running and falling, but picking himself up, pushing away any assistance offered by an unwitting soldier. He staggered against the well in the courtyard and pointed his own shaking hand my way. Amazingly, he smiled serenely as our gazes met.

Was the man truly inhuman? I wondered. His appearance only fueled my conviction to reach the dock.

"The prince has the pestilence!" I insisted, turning to them. "Can't you see how delirious he is? You must let us pass!" I could spy a slice of the ocean through the gatehouse arch. We were so close.

But the soldiers' stares were wedded to the image of the ambling prince.

"I would do as the princesa commands," a voice advised from the other side of the gate.

The minstrel stepped from the gatehouse shadows to grab each soldier by the neck. He banged their heads together and allowed them to collapse into a congenial heap.

"Gracias!" George squealed. I knew I smiled as the minstrel slapped Henry on the back, as if congratulating his wounds.

Henry's smile was pained but he sounded sincere when he said, "Good to see you, too, Gracias."

"This way," he barked, looking at me with amused approval. He then grabbed George's hand. "Sir Andrew is waiting at the dock. But he can't wait long. The prince must not see him."

Didn't the prince already know that Sir Andrew was on our side—the side of the king? But with the castle gate at our backs, and the prince not far behind, we paused on the cliff only long enough for Gracias to release George's hand.

"Go ahead," he ordered us. "I will meet you at the bottom. I wish a few words with the prince." His dark eyes burned beneath his heavy brows to stall any arguments. Henry nodded at Gracias as if some unspoken words passed between them.

"We best descend," Henry said, clutching his side, where I noticed a bloody mark staining his tunic just below his armored vest. He must not bleed to death, I prayed, as we began to descend the stone steps that were wedged into the mountainside of the castle. Before us, the ocean spread out and sparkled like the king's jewels. Small fishing boats dotted the water like driftwood. One of the king's ships lay anchored at the dock at the bottom of the stairs. The Plantagenet flag whipped petulantly in the wind. But the salt of the sea never smelled so good to me.

"Fifty-two steps to the bottom," George mumbled. "I counted them last time."

Henry, who was in front of us, began taking the steps in twos, despite his tender gait. "We will halve that number, George. For then Gracias can join us all the more quickly," he exclaimed, encouraging us to do the same.

It was then, that I spied Sir Andrew as he stepped from behind a cluster of boulders on the beach. A number of soldiers who had accompanied us on our journey to Castile flanked him. His white hair stood out against his dark green cloak like a gull floating on the ocean. Unwittingly, I waved. Yet he did not wave back. He seemed to be squinting at something over our heads.

I paused on a step to look up, to see Gracias pull his sword from his belt, his back to us as he blocked the top stair. He kept his sword poised in the air as he spoke to someone out of my line of sight. I knew it had to be the prince.

I could not hear Gracias's words, but his manner was calm, as if he were reasoning with the prince that it was best to release us. I assumed the prince was conversing with Gracias when the minstrel stood attentively, almost respectfully, as he nodded as if in agreement.

Is the prince really going to let us go? I was afraid to hope.

Gracias then lowered his sword and turned to the sea, this time giving one nod to us, to Sir Andrew, I supposed, that it was all right—that the prince had promised Gracias our safety.

We were nearly on the beach, joy barely beginning to fill my stomach, when I heard the scream of an arrow as it cruelly rent the air. I knew it hit its mark, as its course was instantaneously silenced. I turned as I heard Gracias inhale sharply and I could not stop myself from crying out as the realization of betrayal twisted the features of his face. He dropped his sword before he tumbled down the steps, his bells jingling as his body hit each stair.

"Gracias!" George and I screamed in unison as his body came to rest, sprawling across the stairs at a point midway to the beach.

"We must help him, Nell!" George then cried at me, pushing me away as he lurched toward the steps, as if he knew I would try to stop him. But I was quick and grabbed him by his sleeve. I did not want George to be the Black Prince's next target.

I looked to Sir Andrew to do something, and for a moment he appeared stricken. But just as quickly, all emotion was wiped from his face.

The words that came out of his mouth pierced my heart. I turned to see the Black Prince at the top of the stairs, a bow in his hands.

"We must take them back, my lord, and try them for treason," Sir Andrew yelled as the prince raised the bow again, placing the arrow's feathered tail in the tightly drawn cord.

The prince did not move, but kept his sight trained on us.

"Don't kill them, my lord!" Sir Andrew implored. "They are more valuable to us alive, as the king will need to see with his own eyes that it is truly Nell that still lives. Let them serve us as lesson to anyone who would dare

pose as the royal family." Sir Andrew glanced at us, then
back to the prince.

I knew that Sir Andrew was never rash. Instead he
usually trod each decision deep into the dirt as he walked
his worry circles, but despite his anxious heart, he was
able to buy us some time by appealing to the prince's
vanity. Even if I was an imposter, serving at the prince's
pleasure, he knew the prince would be pleased to make
me suffer for my audacity in thinking that I could mas-
querade as the princess without him. It would not matter
to the prince that I had protested the guise ever since the
princess's death.

The prince lowered the bow and cocked his head to
survey the scene before him. A smile skulked across his
bruised, thin face. His eyes became slits.

"Good work, Sir Andrew," he called from his perch.
He was standing now in a regal pose usually reserved for
portraits, despite the stains on his cloak and tunic and the
wildness of his hair. "I should have guessed that you
would have been one step ahead of me as we untangled
this conspiracy. I will tell the king you served him well as
we send these three through Traitor's Gate." His smile was
gone, his face was grave, and for the first time I could
remember, he looked at me with true hatred in his eyes.

the tower

ON OUR JOURNEY HOME we did not have straw pallets or blankets to soften the unforgiving, splintery deck of the hold. The Black Prince made sure of that. We each had an ankle in shackles, giving us enough space to stand or pace to keep ourselves warm and to keep us alive until we reached the Tower. The prince had stripped me of the princess's dress, which I had dirtied and torn during our flight through the woods. I was wearing some servant's cast-off tunic now. Henry had lost his armor and sword. Only George still wore the worn black tunic that he had donned at the beginning of our journey.

We shared the hold with the princess's numerous trunks. When George and Henry slept during the day, I found comfort in touching her things. They made me feel one with the princess again. How different all of our lives would be if the princess had lived. *Is life on earth ever just?*

During our first dark night in the hold, for our nights were black as we were not provided torches to hold back the rats or sea spirits, George used his healing power to bring Henry back to health. We held hands as we listened to George hum tunes that reminded me of the ocean's sigh as our ship sliced through its surface—not quite living tunes but not of the dead either. When George was finished, I could hear the rise and fall of Henry's chest, the breaths he took to keep alive.

He called out my name once in a fever. "Nell." I squeezed his hand until he quieted.

"I think he cares for you, Nell," George said. I caught the glisten of his eyes in the dark.

"And I for him, George," I replied, feeling a rush of warmth in my face. I was glad that it was dark. "He was a bit cocky at first, but he seemed to come around," I noted quietly.

But George did not know how to shy away from the truth.

"All soldiers are boastful, Nell. It's their way. But Henry decided to stay with us and protect us. Just like a parent or a betrothed would," he said softly.

A *betrothed*. The notion seemed ridiculous, as we had spent our last weeks running from such a promise, but the idea of Henry in such a role surprisingly touched my heart.

"Do you think much about our parents, George?" I asked, as we had finally had the time to call our past to mind. In the darkness, without other people or things to demand the attention of our senses, I could see my mother's and father's faces perfectly.

"I talk to them, Nell. All the time. It's the only way I can bear their absence. I think it is they who enable me to heal people as a way to heal my own heart."

I held back a sob as I pulled him close to me. I had been wrong in believing that I had carried the burdens of our past alone.

The next morning I was glad to see the color in Henry's face restored and the combat return to his brown eyes. As I stared at his full face, I was surprised that I had not realized before quite how handsome he was. George gave me a shy smile and looked away. But later, as the days passed and we neared the end of our ten-day journey, I wondered why he made Henry whole again. To better face his death?

I had asked him this question a few days later, just before dawn, while George was still sleeping on one of several old cloaks that Sir Andrew had found stored on the ship for the king's army. Sir Andrew had been surprised, and I think pleased, to see that we had refused to pilfer any of the princess's possessions for our own warmth or comfort. I awoke to find Henry sitting against the hull, a cloaked wrapped around his shoulders. He was staring at me.

There was a question I wanted to ask but I held back. I was nervous and shy when it came to my feelings for Henry, ever since George and I had spoken of him as one of us.

I did not get up, but instead wrapped my own cloak around my body as I looked into his face.

"Henry," I asked softly. "You are a soldier. What will happen to us when we reach London? I fear for George …and for us," I added with a whisper.

He tilted his head quizzically. The ends of his tangled brown hair touched his shoulders. I could see his eyes glistening in the graying darkness.

"I'm not quite sure, Nell," he replied. He breathed in deeply, causing his shoulders to rise and fall. "The soldiers that I have seen arrested for treason arrived quickly on

Tower Hill. I don't believe that they received much of a trial before their hangings, at least that is what the other soldiers told me." He turned his head away from my vision for a moment, before his gaze returned to my own. "I never had much of a stomach for those sort of things. But you and George are not soldiers," he added quickly. "The king should grant you an audience."

"Let us pray that you are right, Henry. The king is indeed a good man."

We both went silent, until I could no longer contain the question that nagged at my heart.

"Why are you with us, Henry? Why did you risk your life to be with George and me?" Much of the question I mumbled into my cloak. I was suddenly shamed by my presumption of his feelings, despite what George believed.

But then he gave me a warm smile. "You are beautiful, Nell," he said, looking into my eyes in such a way as if it were safe to do so for the first time.

"And you seemed …different…in an exciting way," he added. "Not just because you looked like the princess, but because you were so independent, or maybe it was stubborn, in the way you protected George." His voice lost its gravity and he hugged his knees to his chest like a boy. "When we went chasing George through Portsmouth, I realized that this was something that a real princess would never do. But a real girl with a brave and noble heart *would*. She would trust her heart and not be bound by the rules of royalty."

I knew my face had flushed, but the warmth I felt throughout my body was agreeable. "I am not royal, Henry, as you know too well. George and I were nothing but paupers when the king found us."

Now it was as if a shadow crossed his face. He leaned forward to grab my hands from beneath my cloak, pulling me up so that our faces were close. "This was the other thing, Nell. That day…when I came with the death cart to take your parents away. I was dead in my own heart then," he whispered, peering into my face, as if to find any signs of horror or fear.

"Until George kicked me." He paused and directed a gentle smile at George's sleeping form. "I hadn't been thinking of the bodies that we carried away as people. I couldn't," he insisted. "Not if I was going to keep my wits about me. But then you and George insisted on following me, insisted on knowing that your parents would be properly taken care of…"

"But the king interrupted us," I reminded him.

"Yes," he agreed. "But he did not calm my heart,

which you and George battered to life again. I was not much older than you that day, but it was then that I became a soldier for the king and pledged to look after all in his household."

I was not sure if the shock in my heart showed on my face. Henry had become a soldier to look after George and me, ever since that incredible day in London?

"Yes," he said, nodding as he read my face. "I was alone, too, and you both managed to capture my soul."

We grieved for Gracias, too, but Henry felt the most guilt. He said he was jealous and suspicious of Gracias, probably more jealous than anything else, he admitted. I did not trust Gracias either, I confessed. He was strange and large and had wild hair like an animal. He had a noble heart, George added, and then we went silent. It was curious how easily we bared our hearts in such a hostile and doomed-filled setting. Yet we knew our time was waning.

Sir Andrew brought our food during that first week— brown bread and water and porridge that he scrounged from the cook's kettle. He would pace in his circles around us as he tried to divine a solution to our dilemma.

"I cannot argue against the Black Prince, Nell," he would say sadly, and continue walking around us in his dizzying circles. "I must find another way to show the king that you are innocent."

"I know, Sir Andrew," I replied, trying my best to be like a princess—magnanimous and brave to the end. Only days later, when he made the same plea, I did not hold back. We were sailing to our deaths. What did I have to gain by maintaining a noble silence?

"It's not fair, Sir Andrew!" I cried. "It is the prince who has maligned the name of the Plantagenets!"

He looked at me sadly as if I was a small child. "The king has always cared for you, Nell. We must pray that when he sees you, he will also see into your heart."

Henry nodded hopefully. "You do wear your goodness on your face, Nell, just as George keeps it on the tip of his tongue. Let us pray that the Black Prince's words do not place a veil in front of the king's vision."

The boat pulled back and forth, back and forth, in rhythm with the two oarsmen who kept their steady pace on the Thames. Their faces were hard, cut by lines made by the sun and lifelong labor. Their beards and hair were rough. One growled that we best not talk.

The prince had wasted no time in disposing of us and set us in a ferryboat before our ship had even docked. Our hands were shackled. He spared us the hoods, unlike the poor man that I had seen from the docks before we boarded the ship to Bordeaux three month back. We too were on a final journey to Traitor's Gate. I remember thinking that at least in Castile, I would not have to worry about George being sent to the Tower for his childlike ways I feared he would never lose. The simple truth was always on George's tongue. But now we were being taken to the Tower on someone's lie, a royal lie that would be impossible to protest.

It was drizzling, and the cool mist on my face chilled me. These gray, damp November days in London number more than those blessed with sun. From my vantage point on the Thames, I did not see the normal throng of people moving about their business along the banks of the river. The tradesmen should be rolling their wooden barrels of mead to the pubs or carrying their baskets of fruit and fish, or the women selling still-warm loaves of bread from their tunic aprons. And the children of the docks were usually everywhere, bursting between the alleys of the houses and shops that lined the embankment.

But not today. I barely spied a soul. Even the river was remarkably empty—a large open pond without the traffic of fishing and ferryboats. All I could hear was the cry of the gulls.

The gulls don't get the king's plague, I realized.

So the Black Death *had* reached London.

I was exhausted. Terror can be overwhelming. I looked into George's blue eyes and they were oddly vacant. His blond hair was matted with the dirt and sweat of our past weeks.

"George," I whispered but he did not look at me. He was already far away.

But Henry did and his eyes were full of anger. He was restless and kept shifting his weight in the boat. One of the oarsmen slapped him.

"Stop that! You will turn us all over!" he yelled.

And we will all drown, I thought. No doubt a nicer fate than the one that awaited us.

All too quickly, we approached the tunneled entrance to Traitor's Gate. It looked like the dark mouth of the river sucking us in. Our oarsmen paused, allowing the river to ease us beneath the raised spiked gate.

Two soldiers, knee-deep in water, stood on the other side of the river wall and used their hands to guide our boat into the entry of the arched stone cell built on top of the castle's moat. It was cold and damp in this three-walled room, and I swore I could smell the fear of the hundreds of souls who had made this same journey before us. I wondered if our fear, too, would cling to the air long after we left this place.

George made a nervous sound and I grabbed his hand, the chain on my wrist slapping against my leg. Henry said nothing, but his eyes were shining as he looked around the room, searching for a way out. No one had yet to escape the Tower once they passed through Traitor's Gate.

The soldiers pushed the boat to the set of stone stairs that led out of the moat to St. Thomas Tower and the second set of walls that surrounded the castle. The white-stoned Tower loomed beyond those walls, and the banner of the Plantagenets flew from each of the Tower's four turrets. This is where we were to spend our first night—in the dungeon of the king's keep.

"Out of the boat, girl, and up the steps," one of the soldiers ordered. He barely had a wisp of a beard. I stood up shakily, as my legs had been cold and were numb. One of the oarsmen impatiently pulled me up by the elbow.

"Don't touch her!" Henry yelled, jumping up and causing the boat to rock.

One of the oarsmen cursed.

"Too late to be the hero, boy," the older soldier jeered. "Consider yourself blessed," he added, almost thought-fully. "At least this death will be a swift one. The pestilence can work on you for days."

We did not sleep that night. I kept thinking how

strange it was to be locked in the dungeon of the keep—the White Tower of our king. As a favored servant of the princess, I had been given relatively free reign to roam this castle's halls. Trying to conjure again what was now a foreign sentiment, I remembered that George and I had felt safe here. But now I felt anger and a simmering resentment of the Black Prince.

When we had visited London with the princess, George and I had slept in the servants' quarters of the keep—quarters reserved for those closest to the royal family, and not in the general quarters on the other side of the green. Although the treasury was off-limits to me, as the king kept the royal jewels there, I was permitted to spend as much time as I desired in the Tower's chapel, a room that sparkled with its own multihued glass. The chapel always lifted my spirits. The only other place in the Tower that I never dared venture was the dungeon, where the cries of lonely prisoners could be heard while the rest of the castle slept. I had said many prayers for those prisoners. *Who will pray for us?*

The dungeon was much smaller than our ship's confining hold. Its cobwebbed walls seemed to lean toward us like brooding shadows, hungry to snuff out the tiniest whiff of hope. Rusty torch brackets pockmarked the walls like wounds, and thick, tarnished chains and shackles hung limply like the lifeless bodies they once held.

A pile of old straw in one corner of the room was the only amenity. A latrine in a particularly dank corner introduced the aroma of the moat into the already stifling air. Carvings in the stone-block wall, made by the prisoners before us, were the sole entertainment. As straw was the only commodity here, we guessed that the desperate prisoners made use of their meal spoons to confirm their existence when they feared that no one would see them again. "Though some probably used their rings," George pointed out, placing his fist against the dusty wall and mimicking how one would carefully gouge a mark into it. This was how we kept ourselves occupied, waiting for some word of our trial, as so many prisoners before us.

It seemed that hours had passed by the growl of our stomachs, when we heard the squeal of the solid dungeon door as it opened slowly into our jail. The air of the room was thick, and it seemed to weigh heavily on movement and sound, as if even the air never escaped.

Henry jumped up. "Get behind me, Nell," he instructed.

But the thought of a visitor dampened all reason. Perhaps it was Sir Andrew with some news, I thought hopefully.

But it was the king's imposing form that ducked through the truncated opening.

Henry and George immediately dropped to their knees.

"My lord," they whispered in unison.

I gasped before dropping to my own knees. I did not trust myself to manage a curtsy.

I drew in a breath when I looked at the king. His thick red hair and beard were streaked with the white of age, and his once-full, strong face appeared sunken. Yet he stood tall, and the red mantle emblazoned with the Plantagenets' yellow lions still draped fully from his powerful shoulders.

"Get up, Nell. I need to look into your face," he said.

I stumbled to my feet and self-consciously tried to wipe the dirt from my cheeks and smooth my tangled hair.

"Don't," he ordered. "Say nothing," he added, threat and pain intertwined in his voice. "I only need to look into your face."

It felt like hours, although we must have stared for only minutes at the shadows that devastation had worked into our faces—the king's at the loss of the princess, and my own at our impending deaths based on the prince's false claims. I wondered if he saw the princess in my form, despite my pauper's dress. Did he feel her death more keenly because of my survival, I wondered. How would I have felt, looking into the eyes of a woman who stared back at me with my mother's face?

His eyes hardened as he clenched his fists. I knew my face showed only shame and the misery that he would take to be born from deception, but he would not allow me to tell him otherwise.

"Enough," he finally yelled as he grabbed at the end of his cloak, whipping it around his body as he exited through the door. The yellow lions on the back of his cloak seemed to mock us with their one-eyed stares just before the dungeon door slammed behind the king.

George and Henry immediately scrambled to their feet. George grabbed my arm. "Nell, what did the king want?" he asked, his clear blue eyes telling me that he already knew. "Do you think he saw your heart?" he whispered.

I turned away from George, as the dread on his face was crushing. I had failed. The king, I was sure, saw nothing in my countenance but shame.

"What do you think he saw, Henry?" I asked.

Henry stiffened, as if hurt by the ill-shot accusation in my voice. He tried to take my hand but I pulled it away.

"It's not your fault, Nell," he insisted. "The king has been poisoned by the false words of the prince. Perhaps he is in too much pain to recognize a pure heart."

I seized the sob in my throat before it could tell George that all was lost.

We sat silently for a while. Each of us had claimed a spot along the wall opposite of where the arrow loops allowed slants of sun to touch the floor. How could I get word to the king that I needed to speak to him again—to beg him for one more chance to explain our entrance through Traitor's Gate? The anguish in his eyes had numbed my tongue. I could not cobble together even a feeble protest as he looked upon me as one who would cut a heart like a rope that binds too tightly. But I had George's life to plead for—and Henry's, too. Neither of them were seasoned enough for death.

It was just as the sun was setting and the dungeon began to glow with the last of the dying light, that its door was flung open with a jarring urgency.

This time it was Sir Andrew, with a torch in his hand and an elderly servant behind him, bearing a tray with three bowls.

"I've brought you some refreshment," he announced hopefully. He sniffed distastefully as he entered the room, his watery blue eyes squinting at the contrast between the blaze of his torch and the duskiness of our confines.

The three of us practically tackled Sir Andrew at once, causing him to stumble on the hem of his dark blue cloak. The servant, an old woman in a worn tunic and gray hair plaited above her ears, quickly placed the tray on the floor and fled. The tiny tendrils of steam rising from the three bowls filled the space she occupied seconds ago.

"Sir Andrew, what can you tell us?" I asked, giving him a perfunctory curtsy. When death looms, manners seem suddenly less important.

"The king was here," George chimed in, giving Sir Andrew his gap-toothed smile.

Henry rested his hands on George's shoulders. He looked so frail beneath Henry's strong grasp. "We don't think this was a friendly visit, sir," Henry added as he stared into Sir Andrew's ruddy face.

"It was not," Sir Andrew agreed, immediately combing a hand through his unruly white hair. "I want you all to sit down and eat your stew, while I share with you our latest challenge."

"I'm not hungry," George replied, but as I sat, I yanked him down beside me.

"You'll need your strength," I scolded.

Sir Andrew nodded as we each propped a bowl from the tray on our laps.

"There will be no trial, Nell." He addressed me as if I was the leader of our notorious band.

"No trial?" I repeated.

"Why?" Henry interrupted. "What has happened?"

"The Black Prince has happened, soldier," Sir Andrew replied, walking toward the arrow loops in the wall and listening for a moment, as if the prince's ears were every-where. He placed the torch into one of the brackets and pulled his cloak tightly around his shoulders and shivered. Surely a chill born from horror, as the air in our dungeon chamber was probably warmer than the night.

"There's not even a cord of wood in here!" Sir Andrew protested. "How is one expected to spend their final days in dignity without the slightest of furniture?" he asked, the trembling blaze of the torch lending a fire-touched tinge to his frizzy white hair. "When the Duke of Salisbury was here a few months ago, he had enough chairs to entertain a small party."

"Perhaps the duke later burned the chairs," George offered, pointing to a blackened portion of the floor in one corner. "Just to keep warm."

Sir Andrew nodded. A sad smile played beneath his watery blue eyes. "Perhaps, my boy."

"Sir," Henry interrupted, placing his bowl on the

floor beside him before he stood to join Sir Andrew beneath the torchlight. "Are you trying to tell us that we are doomed?"

Henry's lingering question sent a chill down my spine as we held our breath, waiting for Sir Andrew's reply.

"Finish your stew, and I will continue," he promised. He crossed his arms and watched as the three of us raised our bowls to our lips and gulped the remaining broth.

He nodded approvingly as George wiped his mouth with his sleeve. Weeks ago, before Portsmouth, I would have rebuked him, but if George could live forever with such "common" manners, as the prince once snidely called them, I would ask for nothing more. Sir Andrew seemed to read my mind.

"I won't allow it to happen, Nell, despite the lies that the Black Prince has whispered into the king's ears. His vicious tales have roiled the king's turbulent soul," he whispered his reply past Henry's shoulder.

"What has happened, sir?" I asked, my heart now threatening to burst from my chest.

Sir Andrew took Henry by the shoulder and pulled him close to George and me, until the three of us huddled beneath his pained gaze.

"The prince has convinced the king that a trial is

unnecessary, as the Black Prince himself was witness to your treason." Sir Andrew spit out the last word with contempt. "Besides," he added, "the prince also pointed out that since there would be so few witnesses to the trial, due to the savagery of the pestilence, it would be but a waste of the king's time to host a trial that will end on Tower Hill. The prince would rather see you lose your heads on the green than hang on a deserted hill." Sir Andrew paused and looked deeply into my face. "Tomorrow morning is his preferred time."

"Tomorrow?" I repeated in horror. George's eyes were mooned as he clutched my hand. "Are you sure, sir?" I cried, grabbing both George's and Henry's arms to steady myself. "The king said nothing to us today," I insisted, praying that Sir Andrew might be confused.

"His eyes looked haunted today, Nell," Henry said, glancing at Sir Andrew as if to confirm his reading of the king. "He seemed to be searching your face as if he expected to hear the princess speak through you. He appeared incapable of addressing *you*, Nell."

Sir Andrew nodded. "The king is a shattered man, Nell. He has lost his daughter and half his kingdom. The prince knows how to prey on the weaknesses of good souls." Sir Andrew peered again at the arrow loops. "His creatures are everywhere," he added nervously, his nose wrinkling in disgust.

"Do you mean his rats, sir?" Henry asked, striding over to one of the wall openings to thrust his hand through. He snorted in disgust. "Surely we must tell the king about this evil," Henry insisted. "This goes well beyond the prince's scheme to be rid of the three of us."

"What are we to do, Sir Andrew?" George piped in. "Do you have a plan?" The trust in George's open features forestalled my own skepticism.

"I do, my son," Sir Andrew replied, resting his veined hand on George's head. "It is refreshing to be judged a capable man."

Capable would not protect Sir Andrew's own life, I realized, if the king or the Black Prince saw Sir Andrew entering the dungeon. I did not want one more life on my soul.

"Sir Andrew, I trust you came here unobserved? The servant won't give you away, will she?" I asked nervously. "You have already risked your life for us many times over." Again I felt overwhelmed by the persistent goodness of people despite the wanton evil practiced by the Black Prince. I did not know how to protect anyone, except to protest their innocence along with my own.

"I am safe, Nell," he replied, cupping my chin in his freckled hand to give me a smile. "But, my children," he continued, gathering us around him once again as if truly we were a part of his brood, "you will have to trust that I am working on a solution, and in the meantime, by dawn, make your amends with God in case I am defeated."

When we were first left alone, the three of us searched every crack and crevice in the stone walls for a weakness. Of course none were found. George even tried probing the dirt floor of the prison for a trapdoor, reasoning that some prisoners languished in the Tower for so long that they might have had time to dig a tunnel. Henry and I watched him, not wanting to discourage his blessed distraction.

Exhausted by fear, I finally relented and gathered some of the rotting hay to make a bed not far from the dungeon door. Its dust tickled my nose and its stalks scratched my skin as I pushed a small pile against the wall. I did not plan to sleep but the thought of just sitting for a while seemed overwhelmingly pleasant. As soon as I settled, with my back against the wall and my knees pulled beneath my chin, just as I used to sit as a small girl, Henry plopped beside me. Together we watched George and his erratic shadow as he worked beneath the timid light of our sole torch, looking for clues in the prisoners' carvings.

The thought that this might be our last night in the world jolted me from my respite. Why were George and I born to a life that could promise us nothing? We had lost our parents, our house, really everything that could provide love and protect us. And even when the king allowed us to join his household, there was never really any guarantee that we could stay there. All we had to do was disgrace ourselves or commit some slight, and we would have been on the London streets again. But the princess *did* love us, though that one thought was not enough to temper my pain and anger.

"What are you thinking, Nell?" Henry asked, squeezing my knee to get my attention. "I wish that I could offer you some solace, but I fear that, for the moment, our salvation rests in Sir Andrew's hands."

But Henry couldn't provide me with comfort. My emotions were bound with the prince.

"Why is he doing this to us, Henry? How could he hate us so much?" I asked, my voice threatening to crack.

"We broke from him, Nell. We dashed his dreams of commanding Castile through your marriage, remember? I don't believe any prince would have taken kindly to that."

Henry almost made me smile. "You know what I

mean." I tried to sound peevish. "But what we did was for the good of all. The prince should see that," I argued.

Henry shook his head. His brown eyes softened as he looked into my own. "I no longer believe that being a prince or king makes you a good man. That seems to come from within."

"Perhaps," I agreed, watching George as he now stood directly below the torchlight, using his metal spoon to carve something into the wall. I still had a nagging question for Henry.

I asked keeping my gaze on George. "Why are you willing to die with us, Henry? Would you have joined us in the beginning, when we ran from the prince with Gracias, if you knew that this would be our end?" I held my breath, in case he could not answer.

Then I felt his strong hand clasp my own.

"That's hard to say, Nell, truthfully, although I think I would have gone with you and George no matter what I believed then. Who of us has the power to bargain for anything in this life, Nell? We live by the whim of the crown. With you—"

"Do you truly believe that?" I demanded. Suddenly it was so important that he spoke from his heart.

"Yes!" he exclaimed, placing his other hand gently

under my chin to force me to look into his face. It was dirty and scratched yet still filled with his rough beauty.

"With you," he went on, his voice revving with emotion, "I had the chance to choose my own destiny, to live or to die with a beautiful girl whose spirit and heart matched none that I ever knew in their courage and goodness."

He paused. His eyes were full and his features softened, as if touched by the confidence born of love. I pulled him to me in a fierce embrace and felt his protective arms around me. Why would fate tease me in such a way? To give me a taste of love only to snatch it away the next morning?

"Look, Nell. Look, Henry," George encouraged shyly, bringing me back to the moment. He gestured to the wall behind him.

He had carved:

Forever loyal servants to Princess Joan

Adding the first letter of each of our names as our signature.

"That is beautiful, George," I said and I truly meant it. It did not ease my fear of the morrow, but it did make me feel worthy of the king's trust. We loved the princess, and I should not be ashamed to assert this to the king, especially if the chopping block were the sole obstacle between us.

treason

W E WERE SUMMONED AT DAWN. The two soldiers who had met us at the gate now
led us by our chains up the narrow spiral
stairway from the dungeon to the Tower Green. It was a
cold, gray, November day, the sky the color of worn river
rock. "Bloodless," my mother used to say, because days like
these had drained the color from our cheeks. The memory was mocked by our destination.

The grass between the servants' chapel and the cobblestone square was lush from the fall rains, as was the
field of grass between the square and the castle's crenellated inner walls. The damp blackness beneath their arches
chilled my heart. The moat prowled beneath these walls.
I could smell the tang of its refuse in the air as it mingled

with the aroma of wet grass. Our last breaths were to be filled with portents of death.

As we walked from the Tower to the square, I stumbled once as if I had suddenly walked straight into a wall. Yet nothing was in my path. Instead it was as if the world were hurling every noise and smell, every sight and taste that it had ever offered me, all in one blast that buffeted me like a thunderclap. The smell of the grass and moat pinched my nose and the odors of my companions and the soldiers who prodded us with their swords seemed to wrap around my face like a long-stored veil released from its trunk.

I was aware of the squish of the ground and the scrape of my feet against the stone. My heart seemed to quiver, as if the mingling sounds of distant church bells and lonely gulls were a tune unknown to my ears. But it was the crystal hues of the world that the damp dawn seemed to offer my vision—the raw blades of grass, the grainy brown of the castle's stones, George's startling blue eyes— that caused my own to tear and blur. The world never seemed so alive as this morning.

I looked to George and Henry to see if they were similarly assaulted, and indeed their faces appeared to greet the scenes around us the way a starving man might eye a steaming plate. This morning was to be our last and our spirits seemed hungry to sniff and lap at whatever touched our senses.

Would it hurt, I wondered, as my gaze locked onto the object in the square? Surely George's tiny neck would offer no resistance to the ax, but the thought revolted me. *Please, God,* I begged. *Please, Mother and Father. Can you see us?* I wanted to scream. *Can you make something happen that will stop this madness?* I suddenly felt such shame as I remembered my mother in her final sickness, grabbing my hand and promising me that God would watch over us. Perhaps this was fate. Perhaps God was tired of keeping his eye on George and me and decided that it would be better for us to be reunited with our parents. Maybe I should whisper this notion to George. He would sense its truth better than I.

We had arrived. The tall, bony soldier shoved Henry to the front, causing him to stumble over the chains that hung from his wrists. Henry gave him a look full of poison. The squat older soldier with the pockmarked face snorted a laugh, causing me to wonder anew how people could live without a soul. He pulled at George to yank him between Henry and me. George gave a little yelp as he tried to kick the soldier.

"That's right, George. We will fight them to the end," I said, attempting to rally our spirits against the object now occupying the space before us. The soldier snickered again and spit at our feet.

The polished wooden block commanded the center of the stone-paved square, despite its size. Now that I stood directly in front of it, as I had made sure in the past that George and I never approached it, I could see the half moon shelf carved into its surface. The curve of its bowl was soft, as if offering a gentle rest to a doomed head. But the long, thin handle of the ax that rested against it belied any kind intent.

Henry shifted his stance, blocking our view. "Don't let him look at it, Nell," he said, shaking his head. "It can do no one any good to taint one's mind with such a scene. When we go to battle, we never think of the weapons that each man holds, but of only the men. Men are made of blood, and can thus be defeated."

Can they? I wanted to ask, but remained silent as a light drizzle suddenly touched my face, the mist clinging to my hair and eyelashes. Its clammy, spidery touch set off chills in my already trembling body.

"Did you hear what Henry said, George?" I asked, wrapping my arms around his trembling waist. I could feel the bones beneath his fragile chest.

"Yes, Nell," he answered, his voice punctured by fear, I was sure. "I don't want to die," he said, "but I'm thinking about Mother and Father. In my mind, I can see them with their arms open to us." He sobbed and I held him more tightly. I could taste the bile in my throat. I could not allow this.

"Stand quiet," the soldier with the barely bearded chin ordered us, touching the hilt of his sword, as if to show us that he meant what he said. We were to do nothing but stand there as the few surviving servants of the castle began to trickle from their quarters on the other side of the green. We stood stoically in our cluster on the edge of the chapel's green, Henry first, with George sandwiched between us. Henry's back was erect, his shoulders square, as if to protect us from malevolent stares from the keep and from the shock of the block. The prince had spent the night here, too.

Not one of the king's servants looked directly at us, though I recognized a number of them with whom we had shared the last few years of our lives—during our time with the princess. They began gathering directly opposite us, in a single line, with their backs to the Tower's green and the castle walls. There was Mary, of gray hair and eyes, her apron always stained with the remnants of the meals she cooked. Jane was beside her, sniffling and clinging to Mary's hand. Jane was about my mother's age, and she had treated George and me with kindness. There were a few women, and some girls barely older than myself that I didn't recognize. They all shared the hollowed eyes of the young who were terrified of this plague. On the end of the women's line was the servant with the plaited hair who had accompanied Sir Andrew and brought us our soup. *Where is Sir Andrew?* Surely he would come through for us.

The few men who gathered seemed surly. The blacksmith, the stable hand, a few of the king's lesser guards all seemed impatient to be done with this and out of the rain. Many we had known were missing—victims of the pestilence. A few gasped and made the sign of the cross when one of the brooding black ravens that guarded the Tower hopped onto the block and stared at us all with its beady eyes. Many thought the ravens to carry the spirits of those who lost their heads here.

"Away, foul carrion!" Henry yelled, lunging toward the raven while shaking his chains. The raven appeared to glare at Henry before languidly raising its wings to take off. This caused the men to laugh nervously, and they spit over their shoulders in unison.

"We don't need any more bad luck," he whispered to George and me as he watched the bird alight on one of the Tower's turrets. I could only nod my agreement.

The light rain had stopped by the time King Edward and the Black Prince arrived on the green. I held my breath as I watched the royal guard, each soldier holding one wooden handle that extended from the legs of the king's chair, carry him gingerly, as if the king were in a foul mood. His usually erect form was slumped and his graying hair still held the tangles of the bed. He wore the clothes that he had visited us in last night—the blue tunic and red mantle emblazoned with the Plantagenets' yellow lions. The mantle lay across one leg as if he had carelessly sat in his chair. Unlike his guards, he wore no armor, and his head lacked a crown. I did my best not to look at the prince.

The executioner, wearing black boots, tunic, and stockings, followed the knights. A black mask covered his eyes, which appeared startlingly blue as they peered through the cloth's eye slits. He picked up the ax with both hands, as if its weight required his full strength. He gave it a practice swing.

My heart began to shudder and I placed my hand on my chest to still it. *Where is Sir Andrew?* I looked down the path, towards the Tower's door that emptied onto the green. I turned to look toward the servants' quarters, and then searched the arches of the castle's walls for a glimpse of him. He was nowhere to be seen.

Henry and George had the same question in their eyes. *Surely Sir Andrew will not desert us now?*

Not a word was said as the guards lowered the king's chair, directly opposite us on the other side of the square, in front of the line of servants. The raven called and its cry echoed despairingly against the castle's walls. The servants curtsied and bowed nervously, stepping back to give the king and his son ample space. I felt weak-kneed when I finally met the gaze of the prince.

I could hear nothing for the moment but the blood coursing through my head. The prince was wearing his black cloak and the pointy boots he favored, which curved like serpent's tongues at their tips. A gold crown studded with bloodred rubies rested on his head. I realized that in France he had preferred the hood of his cloak but he was home again, in the presence of his king, and today, unlike the king, he bore the crown. The prince nodded slightly as he gave me a satisfied smile. His black eyes held the cold of winter.

I drew in a breath when I looked at the king. He

appeared as he did yesterday, tired and defeated by age and tragedy, yet his eyes seemed to burn with an unmitigated anger. I prayed that this fury was not reserved for us. He drew his mantle across his broad chest as he stood, waving the guards away from him. He stared at us but addressed the Black Prince. "Shall we get on with it?" Disgust laced his words.

"Indeed," the Black Prince replied, raising his pointed beard in our direction. He rubbed his hands in apparent anticipation. A smile slithered across his face. He motioned to the pockmarked guard at our side. "Undo their chains," he commanded, his words rising in a tease.

One of the soldiers motioned for us to extend our hands. He unlocked the shackles from our wrists and they fell to the ground in a metallic thud. The soldier then pulled Henry from our midst and shoved him toward the block.

"Yes," the prince approved. "I want to save the churl for last."

"Henry!" I cried. George attempted to break away. He kicked and screamed when the soldiers grabbed him. The women servants let out cries of their own. They seemed to have no more stomach for death.

"Mercy, my lord!" Jane, the servant who had treated

us like her own children, implored the king. Her mouth was trembling. Mary, the cook, grabbed her arms. "They are barely grown." Her words, a faint whisper, seemed magnified in the damp air. All gathered seemed to hold their breath.

The Black Prince turned on her, as if to strike. The king stayed his hand.

I felt faint with terror, but with this diversion, I managed to slip from the guards to approach the king.

"My lord," I said, closing my eyes to force the tears back as I curtsied.

The king said nothing. He stared at me as if searching my features—my eyes, my hair, my mouth. For a moment I thought he might reach out to touch me. Me, the girl who still walked on this earth, daring to look like his daughter. His chin trembled so slightly that I believed only I could see the rush of emotion in his face. I wondered if he was thinking of that day many years ago, when he thought I would be useful in protecting his daughter. But the pestilence was no regular enemy. It was willing to take the life of a princess just as easily as that of a pauper.

"Nell," he finally said, his voice firm. "I do not understand."

"Nor I, my lord," I said, my voice faltering with the

pain I shared with him. "I don't know why the princess was taken instead of me."

I was not sure if that was what he was asking me, but I could not speak against the prince, not yet. Not while he still held the king's grief in his hands.

"Shall I speak on your behalf, Nell?" Henry called out from behind me. "I was a witness to it all, my lord," he shouted. His voice was strong. I turned to see him straining against the guards who held his arms.

George squeezed past them. "I can speak, too, my lord, for Nell has always been good to all people." One of the guards swiped at him with a gloved hand, but George ducked and stepped away. "She especially loved the princess," he insisted, his eyes filling with tears.

A sob welling in my own throat threatened to silence me. I was blessed to claim such a brother and a friend.

But then the Black Prince stepped between the king and me, shoving me aside with his hand. "Is that why you surrounded her with victims of this plague?" he sneered, seemingly angry that I had the attention of the king. "So that you could take her clothes and servants, so that *you*, not the princess, would become the next queen of Castile?" He sidled beside the king and leaned into my face, his pointed beard inches from my nose. A different fury roiled in his eyes. His fetid breath, like that of an animal's, caused me to falter. I closed my eyes to his terrifying image. "The temptation must have been irresistible, even for one who pledged her life to protect the princess." The words he whispered into my ears had the twist of a knife.

"That is a lie!" Henry shouted. "My lord, you must let Nell speak," he pleaded.

The women servants lined behind the king's chair nodded their agreement. "Yes," they mouthed, grabbing for one another's hands.

I needed to be brave for George and Henry. Incredibly, I pushed the Black Prince away, causing him to stumble back. A delighted smile played on his face, which suddenly infuriated me.

"She did die of the pestilence, my lord! It was all around us!" I protested. The king crossed his arms. His face was inscrutable. "I did not know how to protect her," I added weakly.

The Black Prince turned to address the king, the servants, and the guards, who now huddled behind them. Jane and Mary gazed upon their lords as if their world had gone mad.

"How dare this wench address her king so!" the Black

Prince bellowed, shock feigned by the wideness of his eyes. "Does your lord deserve such disrespect? Of course not!" he answered for them. "That is why they are here to die!"

"The Black Prince is lying, Your Highness," Henry said, in a voice firm and bereft of fear. It seemed that the three of us had crossed some line, where death seemed inevitable and all truths could be said. The servants and soldiers surrounding us gasped. The soldiers yanked at Henry's arms, as if that would stop his speech.

And then the prince's predator eyes locked on Henry. He pulled a knife from the belt around his waist and held it to the air.

I turned to Henry. His eyes were bright and his face severe. He would not heed such a threat. George thrust his arm around Henry's waist and pulled him close. He knew the prince was capable of anything.

My own heart refused to be silenced. I thought of all the people who had risked their lives to save us— Sir Andrew, the priest, the gravedigger, Albert and his brothers—and Gracias and his soldiers, who *did* lose their lives. I knew they were struggling to save England and Spain from a false marriage—one that could have possibly compromised the truce between our countries. But if that was all Gracias was looking to save, why did he come back to Bordeaux? Did I dare dishonor Gracias's memory by remaining silent?

"It was the prince who refused to leave Bordeaux, my lord, even when the mayor warned us that the plague fires were already burning," I said, my voice rising over the din. "After she died . . . I was asked to play the princess. . . ." I stopped. What could I say as to not sully the reputation of his eldest son? There was nothing to be said.

The king leveled his smoldering gaze on my face. *Is all his anger reserved for me?* I wondered. I prayed not.

"I was not privy to the prince's intentions," I finally added, feeling the heated gaze of the king and the prince fully upon my shoulders. "In the end, I was scared and returned to Bordeaux, fearing that I could not live up to the divine qualities of the princess."

I looked into his eyes as I spoke. His eyes, which among all other features bore the only evidence of the howling rage beneath his pale skin. He reached behind his back for his chair, as if he intended to sit. One of the royal guards came to his side to guide him, but he motioned the guard away.

I am nothing like the princess. She would never have embarrassed herself, nor have shamed the king by addressing him in such a manner. Yet he raised his bearded chin to me, and his eyes, suddenly more thoughtful, invited me to continue.

"I could not protect the princess," I cried. "I prayed at her death that it was *I* who succumbed to the pestilence and not your daughter. I loved her, too, my lord, as she was kind to George and me." Despite my efforts, I began to weep.

"Enough!" the Black Prince yelled. "This is treason! I will put an end to this now!"

His voice boomed off the castle's walls. To my eyes, he suddenly seemed to grow, looming many feet taller, beneath the protective shadow of his black cloak. He pulled his sword from his belt, tossing his knife to the ground. "Allow me, sir, to do the honors," he said with a quick bow to his father. All eyes were riveted on the prince.

And then someone screamed. I knew it wasn't me, but it was the scream of a woman. More of the women joined them, as they pointed behind us, toward the White Tower.

I turned to see the creatures, pausing and sniffing at the air as they raised their heads over the rim of the moat, before tumbling onto the land. They moved like soldiers on a sneak attack, running in bunches along the shrubbery that grew beneath the lowest set of windows in the

Tower. They bled out from the Tower like a mud-colored shadow, slinking toward us across the castle's green. Some followed the cobblestone path that emanated from Traitor's Gate. They moved as if they believed they were invisible to us, sprinting, stopping, turning in circles—to ensure that they had not lost our scent. There must have been a hundred of them running in the slick, cruel packs that had occupied my dreams. The rats.

They must have entered through Traitor's Gate—the only living creatures small enough to slip through the watery portcullis and breech the sanctum of the Tower.

"What fresh treason is this?" the Black Prince screamed, raising his sword at me as if I had somehow commanded his vile little army. He then turned to the king, his own vermin-like eyes narrowing. "My lord, is this *your* game?" he asked, his voice straining to remain calm.

The king was back in his chair, as if he found the scene exhausting, yet I noticed that his veined hands gripped the armrests as if at any moment, he might spring at the prince. "No, my son. I believe that Sir Andrew had a finger in this." A guttural growl soaked his words. The king pointed in the direction of the gate.

I glanced toward the gate to see Sir Andrew, in a red tunic and blue cloak, trotting along the edge of the moat toward the stairs of Traitor's Gate, his wild white hair shining like a beacon on this gray day. He held what looked to be a horn in his hand—an ivory horn—like that of a unicorn's used by generals to summon their men to battle.

The scene before us was like a dream, as Henry grabbed my hand and picked George up, holding him in his arms. *Is that what the Black Prince used to muster his rats?* I remembered seeing that horn once before in the hand of the prince as he danced around the bonfires on the beach at Bordeaux. Somehow, Sir Andrew had gotten hold of it and was using the rats to distract or make our plea to the king.

They were everywhere now, a small, vicious army looking to satisfy their battle lust. The rats were leaping onto the backs of the women, climbing up tunics to bite an exposed hand or throat. The women were not armed or protected by armor. Their terrified screams pierced the air. Jane and Mary cowered against the Tower's wall, closing their eyes and screeching at the new horror before them. The younger women seemed to draw the rats as they flailed and kicked at the creatures. The rats' lust for battle seemed to magnify.

It was then that the king came alive.

He stood, slowly drawing to his full height as he snatched the sword of one of his royal guards. "Find another sword, man, and defend the women! All of you! It will not be said that a few rats can scare the king's army!" he roared. He then pointed the sword at the Black Prince, who was scowling peevishly at the mayhem around him. "Allow my son to lead you. I am told that he has experience with such witchery."

The king and Black Prince locked gazes until the prince's sights dropped to the ground. "We will send them back to the moat!" the Black Prince ordered, pushing past the soldiers in front of him with a shove.

Henry pulled me toward the king, lowering George to the ground in front of the king's knees. "If I may leave them with you, my lord, as I find myself a sword to join the fray." The mischief was back in Henry's eyes. *Is he really so confident that we have regained the king's affections?*

The king did not smile, but nodded as he took hold of my hand. He held it fiercely. "Take the sword of one of my ancient guards." He pointed toward an old man in chinked armor, who was stumbling on the cobblestone path as the rats leaped against his legs. "The old are not a match for such evil," he growled.

George and I were huddled beneath the mantle of the

king as we watched the fantastic scene before us. The soldiers bore down upon the rats with an unbound fury, snatching the rats with their gloved hands to thrust them to the ground to stomp and then slice at their heads. The screeches of the frenzied rats mingled with the cries and shouts of the women and soldiers. The smell of blood-tinged dew filled the air. My empty stomach turned. Surely this must be a scene from hell.

The servants had already scrambled, running in all directions, as none seemed an assured escape. The soldiers and royal guards followed, swinging their swords with what looked like a force normally reserved for dragons as the rats charged them with a confidence that belied their small size. They seemed crazed by the blood spilled around them. They wanted more and seemed to think nothing of the cost.

"Hold on to me, Nell!" George shouted as he watched a terrifying pack run across the green.

But the rats did not approach our small group. Instead they cowered when they drew closer, under the curses of the Black Prince, who had by this time returned to the square, furious, his face flushed with heat. "Push them toward the moat," he ordered the pockmarked soldier and Henry, who had the old soldier's sword in his hand now and swooped upon the rats almost gleefully.

Authority blazed in the king's eyes as the prince approached.

"Does my son dabble in the black arts?" he demanded, pushing one of the royal guards away. "Assist the women!" he demanded impatiently, fury welling up in his voice. The armored soldiers scurried after the rats, leaving the king and the Black Prince alone with George and me.

"What do you say? Are these your creatures?" the king pressed. I thought I detected a weariness in his outraged voice.

The prince glanced at me furtively like an animal before answering the king, as if he wanted to make sure that I would not flee. He tightened his grip on his sword as he turned to address the king.

"They are, my lord. I use whatever powers that be to better protect our kingdom. I am not timid about that," he replied proudly. "A pity this latest lot had to be discarded," he added, turning toward the Tower and Traitor's Gate. I followed his line of sight. By this time, the women had taken refuge in the Tower. Only the men and Henry remained on the green. They were herding the remaining rats toward the moat with their boots and swords. By now, the rats' bloodlust was spent as they crawled, their fur sleek with red-dashed sweat. Sir Andrew remained on the steps of Traitor's Gate, supervising the rats' plunge into the waters. He still clutched the horn in his hand.

"Will the rats drown?" George asked. He sounded hopeful.

"Yes, they'll drown," the Black Prince replied, whipping around to face us again. "Sir Andrew will pay for this mess," he added petulantly.

The king shook his head like a disappointed father, without so much as a sideways gaze to inspect the progress of his men as they steered the rats. Their speech, punctuated by nervous laughter, filled the air. They had regained a semblance of victory. The king eased himself into his chair, as if movement were painful again.

"Tell Andrew to come to me," the king ordered. A hungry smile played across the prince's face as he yelled to Sir Andrew to approach. The prince raised his sword as Sir Andrew's colorful, ambling figure drew near. Sir Andrew held no sword. Only the horn, whose powers seemed to have drowned with the rats.

"Hold, my son," he ordered. "Put your sword down, unless you intend to use it to chop a few strays." The prince's arms quivered as he raised the sword above his head, before slamming it down hard upon the empty chopping block.

"My lord," Sir Andrew said, dropping to one knee with difficulty. He was, after all, an old man—an old man who had spent the last hour running along the moat, summoning the rats to just as quickly dispose of them. George ran to his side to take him by the arm.

"Thank you, my boy," Sir Andrew mumbled, leaning on George's skinny frame to pull himself up again. I caught the shimmer of sentiment in the king's eyes, but the prince's eyes were filled with loathing.

"Have you proved your point, sir?" the king asked, as if he and Sir Andrew were in the midst of completing some debate.

"I do believe I have, my lord," Sir Andrew replied, his already ruddy complexion appearing redder beneath his halo of white hair. "Call me treasonous if you must, but I thought the king needed to know that he had a rat in his midst."

"How so, Andrew? That is a charge full of treason." The king cocked his head, awaiting a studied response.

"As you saw, my lord, the rats responded to the prince's battle horn. They respond to none other." Sir Andrew lowered his gaze respectfully.

"And what do you say to this, my son?" the king asked, suddenly locking his gaze on me.

The prince sputtered. He held his sword in both hands now. He was trembling violently.

By now, Henry and the royal guards had rejoined us. I could hear them breathing heavily to regain their wind. Henry grabbed my hand, and I felt a rush of pride. He was just a common-born soldier, but in my regard, he was twenty times the man that the Black Prince feigned to be.

"My lord," the Black Prince cried, sounding truly exasperated. "You would take the word of a servant over that of your son?" The question sounded more like a dare.

"The threads of this story bound you to its vicious core, my son. But what pains me more than your dark pride is your willingness to sacrifice Nell and George to hide your part in this intrigue. We have a pledge to protect the innocents." The king ran his hand across his face, rubbing his forehead as if it truly ached. "I fear that you shall never grow into this throne."

"I shall slaughter them all," the prince said, in a voice that contained a hint of madness.

The king rose swiftly. His guards jumped to attention. "Escort my son to his chambers," the king ordered evenly, "and stay with him there until I am ready to join him.

And the prisoners. . . ." He used the term more gently. "Take them back to the dungeon to wait for me."

Before he turned on his heel, the prince threw us a deadly look. Sir Andrew's eyes fluttered. I prayed that his skittish heart would hold. He had been so brave this day.

We said nothing as we watched a pair of the armored guards shadow the prince's furious gait to the Tower. The Tower green was deserted now. Its grass bore flecks of blood. The early morning sky was a melancholy gray. The Tower's raven was once again perched on the edge of one of the castle's turrets. He would be patient. He cocked his head and watched as we were taken, without chains, back to the dungeon.

journey

IT IS HARD TO DESCRIBE HOPE, but I knew it was the emotion we were feeling as we sat on the straw that had softened our burdens during the night, our backs against the cold, pocked stone of the dungeon's walls. Shabby prisms of light teased their way into the darkness by way of the arrow loops, giving the impression of the netherworld. But still, my heart was lighter than it was when the day had dawned.

I wondered, looking at George's bright red cheeks and ears, *Is this what hope dared to look like?* His blood seemed to have renewed itself, touching his skin from the inside out. Henry looked at me fiercely, as if his vision were suddenly restored from blindness.

"Nell, I believe the king still loves us," George

whispered, leaning forward to see Henry and me. "He sounded angry at the prince for getting us in trouble," George reasoned. He nodded as he spoke, as if the action would convince me by suggestion. His dirty brown bangs brushed against his eyelids.

"That's because he sees the face of his daughter," I said, "although I am nothing like the princess."

Henry replied, a smile softening his features. "The king surely recognizes the loyalty and strength within you."

I bowed my head, wanting to honor and plead for that thought. If only it were so.

"Ah, but you *are* like the princess," a deep voice resonated from the dungeon's entrance. We had not heard the squeak of the wooden door. It was the king.

We pulled one another up, bumping into one another as we curtseyed and knelt clumsily.

"My lord," we said in unison. I was vaguely aware that my knees were trembling.

"Nell, come to me," he commanded softly. His mantle fell from one shoulder as he extended a ringed hand to me. His eyes were warm, the lines in his face more shallow.

"I need you to give me a reason to stay your execution, to believe your word over the word of my own son," he said.

I glanced back at George and Henry, and they smiled and nodded, encouraging me to tell our truths. I knew I had no other choice.

"Forgive me, my lord, for being presumptuous, but I will tell you what I think you need to hear."

From there it was like a falling, words and thoughts tumbling from my mouth and I could not have stopped their momentum no matter how dire and grave they sounded. I told the king everything, from the prince's mysterious appearance on his sister's ship as we approached Bordeaux to the princess's death, and the prince's terrifying dance under the flames of the pestilence pyres on the beach. I told him of the prince's insistence that I play the role of the princess to win the hand of the prince of Castile, our escape from him in the woods, and our journey back up the coast to Bordeaux. I cited those, by name or trade, that had assisted us as we fled the prince's rats. Finally I told him of the betrayal of Gracias. That act had cut me the deepest.

My heart was racing when I had finished, my dry tongue ignorant of how to take my story back to the present. Instead I lowered my head. "I wish I could have saved the princess. She had given me so many gifts—her love and friendship, her home and spirit. And she taught me to read. She shared her knowledge and wisdom with me. She made me feel as if George and I meant something to the world," I whispered. I did not know whether my final words had reached the air. But when I finally had the resolve to look the king in the face again, he was gone.

Before the morning had ended, we had one final visitor, who beckoned us from the dungeon doorway. Although the shadows muted the brightness of his dress, the whiteness of his hair was unmistakable.

"Sir Andrew!" George cried. "Are we allowed to come out?"

"Yes, my boy," he chortled. "And it is just as much a relief to me as to you, as I cannot abide the rank airs of the dungeon."

George jumped up from our straw pallets and threw himself into Sir Andrew's arms. It cheered me to see that his affections had not been tainted by our ordeals. George was truly blessed with a generous spirit.

Henry and I approached the torched light of the hallway a bit more tentatively. I was almost afraid to believe that our horror had ended.

"Have we been pardoned, sir?" Henry asked quietly, as if not wanting to shatter George's joy. He squeezed my hand reassuringly.

Sir Andrew's round, ruddy face seemed to cast its own light. "Indeed you are, my boy. The king has instructed me to ensure that you are bathed and fed, and provided with some clean and warm clothes for your journey."

My joy was muted by the moment's trepidation.

"Our journey?" I repeated, searching Sir Andrew's eyes for some clue. "Has the king decided to send us on an errand?"

Sir Andrew shook his head. His arms still encircled George's tiny frame. "No, my dear. The king simply wants to ensure your safety."

I must have looked confused, because Henry, too, cocked his head before asking the question that made too clear our situation.

"What will happen to the Black Prince, sir?" Henry asked as if he already knew the answer.

Sir Andrew sighed. "Nothing, my boy. The Black Prince is the heir to the throne. The king plans to spend his remaining years actively grooming his son."

"Will you be protected, Sir Andrew?" I asked. He hadn't mentioned embarking on his own journey.

"I will, my dear. The king assures me that the importance of my health will be made clear to the prince, as it is related to his own ascendancy to the crown."

George had been listening intently, despite his boyish calm at this latest news. His face suddenly became serious, his gap-toothed smile replaced by a more mature mien.

"I don't believe the prince will ever become king," George said. "I can feel it in my bones."

Before sunset, we said our good-byes to the king and to Sir Andrew. They never asked us where we might go, and what we intended to make of our future, but when Sir Andrew led us across the Tower's green, toward the drawbridge that led to Tower Lane, it was the king who emerged from the stables, followed by three royal guards, each leading one of the king's horses.

When Henry and George dropped to their knees and I fell into a quick curtsy, I suddenly felt the grasp of a strong hand on my arm and I was pulled into the king's embrace.

"You have honored my daughter, Nell, these past two years more capably than any nobility."

Again I felt the tears that threatened whenever I thought of the princess.

"I loved her so, my lord," I whispered.

"I know," he said as he pressed a purse into my hand.

"You, sir," the king said to Henry. "Will you protect them always?"

"I will, my lord. On my soul, I will do my best."
Henry turned to me to share a slow, reassuring smile.

"Thank you, my lord," I whispered as Henry assisted
me, and then George, into the saddle. Henry quickly was
on the back of his own horse.

I did not know where we would go. I only knew that
we were going away from the prince and from this plague
that had tainted us all. When I took a final glance over my
shoulder, to look one last time at the Tower, I swore I dis-
tinguished the prince's silhouette in one of the high windows of the Tower's royal quarters. For a moment, time
stopped, and I realized that the sudden swooshing that
rang in my ears was the sound of my own pounding
heart. The figure in the Tower leaned into the open air
and then slowly extended his hand to me, as if beckoning
me to join him, just as he did in that long-ago dream. I
could not see his face but I could imagine his scornful
smile. I stared until he turned away and disappeared into
the castle.

"What is it, Nell?" Henry asked, glancing toward the
Tower suspiciously.

"It is nothing, Henry." I attempted a smile. "I was just
thinking how wonderful it is that we have our freedom."

Aldus Manutius, a highly influential Renaissance printer, designed *Bembo* over five hundred years ago in Venice, Italy. He first used the light, easy-to-read type in the late fifteenth century publishing an essay by Pietro Bembo, an Italian scholar. The typeface soon became extremely popular throughout the country. When *Bembo* reached France, famed Parisian publisher and type designer Claude Garamond tried to duplicate it. This caused *Bembo*'s influence to spread throughout the rest of Europe. In 1929, the English Mono-type company revived the *Bembo* design using books and materials set with Manutius' original fonts. By the 1980s, Monotype had created a digital version of *Bembo*, along with semi-bold and extra-bold weights and italics. This latest incarnation has solidified *Bembo* as one of the most prevalent typefaces today.